A Martha y Tom
Matthews cordialmente

[signature]

Nov 1959

THE KING AND THE QUEEN

THE KING AND THE QUEEN

Ramón J. Sender

translated from the Spanish
by Mary Low
The Vanguard Press, Inc.
New York

Sept. 08, 1993

In the winter of 1936 my brother Manuel and I were hunting wild boars in the Sierra de Guara (Aragón). We were on horseback and talking politics.

"If the Fascists rise in rebellion and triumph," he said, "they'll shoot me before they shoot you."

He said so smiling, as too serious things are likely to be said. Shortly afterward the civil war began, and the Fascists triumphed in the provincial capital where he was mayor. Two policemen went to his house and said to him:

"We have orders to arrest you. Go away and we will say we have not found you." My brother Manuel answered:

"There is no reason for me to run away, and I won't go. Arrest me, if you like."

He had a car full of gasoline in the garage, the French border fifty miles away, and on the other side of the border a comfortable home where Francis Jammes, the old poet, frequently spoke to him and his young wife of the sweetness of Christian peace. My brother found it nobler to remain and face the danger with his honest man's quiet smile. He was shot without trial one week later. To him I dedicate this narrative humbly and devotedly.

R. S.

THE KING AND THE QUEEN

CHAPTER
ONE

O N EITHER SIDE OF THE STAIRCASE THERE WAS
a sixteenth-century sedan-chair made of sil-
vered wood and blue silk with Renaissance
embossments on the doors. The coat of arms—three
boars' heads on a gules field—could be seen embroi-
dered on the inner tapestry, with the motto in minute
Gothic lettering: "More for the enterprise than for the
prize." These and other similar details gave to one
part of the palace a certain museum-like aspect, which
the duchess found affected.

The palace had three stories, with a monastic tower
rising two stories higher on the north wing. It was surrounded on three sides by a park, with trees leaning
out over the wall onto a silent alley. In 1928 and '29,
the duke and duchess had held the most sumptuous en-
tertainments of the court in this house. The King and

Queen used to attend them. On those gala nights the building and the park were lit up discreetly. Reflectors hidden among the moldings cast a diffused glow over the parterres, and from the clumps of box came vague glimmers that wrapped the palace in an unreal aura. Rómulo, the porter and head gardener, looked with pride at the great blue carpet covering the steps and stretching out onto the yellow gravel beneath the marquee. And even on top of the carpet there was an ornate strip of white matting that went from the doorway—the full width of the door—to the place where the royal carriage stopped. Several times Rómulo had seen the King, for whose physical presence he had no respect whatever. He seemed to him like a dummy, a mechanical doll with long wooden legs ending in the finest shoes in the world. The parties lasted nearly all night, but the King and Queen left early, and when they had gone Rómulo, the gardener, used to ask the butler to let him put out the park lights, because "those lights at night disturb the trees, the plants, and especially the flowers."

The de Arlanza family was that of the duchess. Her husband was the Duke of Alcanadre, but since they lived in the Arlanza palace everybody went on calling them by this name, which pleased the duchess as a recognition of her family's greater social standing and did not bother her husband. The old duke who held the title had given the house to his daughter and son-in-law, and this meant ceding several millions. Not

4

that generosity was the decisive factor in his character, but the old duke could not live there—for certain reasons he was afraid of the rooms where his wife had died—and moreover he believed he had no right to sell his ancestral home.

The *salle d'armes* was in the basement and had a covered swimming pool in it. That swimming pool—like the elevator which had been put in at the tower—meant a bold novelty in the palace traditions, and the duchess used to go there almost daily to swim for half an hour quite naked. One of the doors of the *salle d'armes* gave onto the park, and the other onto a kind of cloister that enclosed an inner yard. On sunny mornings the high windows cast yellow patches and shadows of green foliage on the warm water of the swimming pool. The duchess amused herself in the pool like a child. Her cries rang out under the vaulting, among the gray stones that shaped the echo and lent it the solemnity of a castle or monastery. Sometimes after undressing she would say: "It's funny how easy it is to strip." She would say this glancing at a lay figure that was used for fencing classes and seemed to be mounting guard over the racks. It was not unusual for the duchess to ask the maid to lift a corner of the armorial hanging that covered one part of the wall. The maid would do so, and nearly always a tiny white moth came flying out. The duchess would feel reassured when she saw there was no one between the hanging and the wall.

5

Opposite the little springboard from which the duchess dived, on the other side of the pool, there was a mirror which reflected her whole body, and staring into it with that suspicious glance women use in looking at themselves she would recall:

"When I was a child I was told that if I looked at myself naked in the mirror I'd see the devil." Since then she had looked at herself many times without seeing him and had come to the conclusion that the devil might be in her own complacent gaze. But she had never been afraid of the devil—"perhaps," she would say, "because he's masculine." Even in her childhood she could not help noticing that the devil was a kind of handsome Don Juan of the church. She had told her confessor one day, at a time when she read a great deal and had a "mania for interpretations":

"I imagine the devil's a good-looking, clever young man. To me he's rather like Apollo must have been to the Gentiles."

Her confessor had laughed and chided her.

The duchess was a well-behaved young lady. In spite of her beauty she had caused no gossip—an unusual thing—either as a girl or as a married woman. This is not to say that she led a conventual life. Being motherless, and with her father absorbed in mistresses and horses, she was given a pleasant freedom of which she made the most by traveling and taking up sports. Little by little she gave up the sports because they

6

made her "too muscular"—at least this was her official excuse to herself—but really because outside Spain "sporting freedom" was understood to have a double meaning in practice, and the duchess hated anything ambiguous. Generally she was accompanied by her aunt, the Baroness of Alcor, who had a passion for journeys. It was on one of these—in Switzerland —that she met Estéban R., Marquis of R. In Madrid he had a terrible reputation with women and resembled the picture the duchess had formed of the devil when she was a child. For both reasons she found him interesting, and for a while they went everywhere together. But Estéban—she told herself—was not so terrible as he appeared. When she realized that he was treating her "differently" because he thought of marrying her, she felt highly disappointed without knowing why, returned to Madrid, and a few weeks later married the Duke of Alcanadre, an amiable, upright man with a great regard for social conventions. The duchess dominated him so thoroughly that she would have considered deceiving him a senseless misuse of authority. On the other hand, the duchess was not a woman of strong emotions.

The duke found no permanent harmony in his wife's character, but a varied interplay of large and small surprises. When these appeared gently, like the changes wrought by natural light in forms and colors, always the same yet always different, he was charmed. But sometimes the duchess had disconcerting habits,

7

and these sudden changes alarmed her husband, who was as much in love with her as a man incapable of passions can be. One day he told her she was a monster, but that he loved her as she was.

The duchess became very serious.

"A lovable monster isn't a monster any more, but a prodigy."

They got on well together because neither of them tried to probe into the depths of the other's feelings. The duchess used to say: "We're an ideal couple because we're not in love."

That July morning in 1936, the duchess was swimming in the pool and thinking that their tardiness in leaving Madrid this summer was beginning to be noticed by their friends and relations. She was swimming completely naked, and her body slid with easy movements between the marble planes of the pool. She was floating motionless on the surface when Rómulo knocked at the garden door. He was a middle-aged man. He had the Roman head of a Cordovan peasant. He spoke little, and his ideas about persons and things were very solid. Like all peasants, he had made up his own philosophy and enjoyed generalizing. He termed life "a muddle of vice-versas," and Rómulo tried to straighten out that muddle by being one of the court's best gardeners. He knocked again, and the maid went to answer. As the door was cut off from the pool—the *salle d'armes* was enormous and formed an angle—the maid opened it. The duchess heard

8

them arguing. The soprano voice of the servant and the gardener's bass made a striking contrast. Rómulo was insisting that the duchess had given special orders. The duchess suddenly intervened, saying:

"Rómulo, come in."

The maid stepped forward.

"My Lady, it's a man."

The duchess raised her eyebrows.

"Rómulo a man?"

She laughed with a brief birdy trill. When Rómulo came in she was still laughing. The maid tried to fold up a towel, but her hands were shaking. Rómulo's voice saying good morning was shaking too. The duchess went on floating on her back, moving her hands and feet slightly. Rómulo, who had heard the duchess' words and the trill which consecrated and sealed her disdain—"Rómulo a man?"—thought that if he averted his gaze from his mistress' body he would be proclaiming the impropriety of the situation, and he remained looking at her unblinkingly and also—it must be said—unseeingly. Having the duchess naked in front of him made him feel like somebody else, and the need of understanding "that other somebody"—which meant a brutal surprise— prevented him from knowing what he saw. The duchess took the envelope Rómulo was holding out to her, opened it, read something on a piece of paper, put the paper back in the envelope, gave it to the maid, and remained looking at Rómulo.

"Was the man who brought the letter a chauffeur of the de M.'s?"

"Yes, My Lady."

"Is he waiting?"

"Yes, My Lady."

"Tell them I'll call up at midday."

Rómulo could not move. Luckily the maid came between them and, by spreading towels along the edge of the swimming pool, breaking up the rigid air in that space where the light seemed to have crystallized, enabled the gardener to shift one foot, attempt to leave, and finally get out. As he walked into the park his head was spinning. He went slowly back to the lodge, looking at his feet and the shadow of his body tied to them. He could not understand anything. Neither the shadow, nor his feet, nor his own dazzled eyes. By the time he reached the lodge, he had forgotten about the people who had brought the letter, but when he saw the car waiting at the gates he seemed to wake up.

Meanwhile the startled maid was showing her fright in every gesture, every glance, every silence. And thinking: "Things happen to the mistress like in dreams!" The duchess noticed and said:

"A gardener isn't a man!"

She turned over sideways and began swimming with long strokes. Then she climbed from the water, took up the envelope again, drew out a telegram, read it once more, and later burned it in a small electric stove on the dressing table. She did not speak. The silence between those walls of marble and Castilian stone had something of a golden aura. In the park, a car could be heard drawing up, and shortly afterward the duke's voice sounded on the other side of the door, asking permission to enter.

"Wait," answered the duchess, reaching for a bathrobe, in which she wrapped herself.

When the duke was allowed in, the maid left discreetly. With a gloomy expression the duke began pacing nervously between the dressing table and the pool.

"I didn't find anybody at home. I think they've all left by now and have gone to their appointed places."

The duchess listened to him with her back turned, intent on the mirror. She looked at herself with the keen, wise glance one uses in looking at a rival.

"I told you before not to bother," she said, "because the news would reach us here."

She pointed to the burnt paper on the marble and said:

"Tomorrow at seven."

The duke was playing a dangerous game, and it was the first time in centuries that the de Arlanzas or the de Alcanadres had risked so much. The duchess watched her husband with discreet curiosity, and from his bearing she quickly guessed both his unshaken resolve and a hint of discouragement. His nerves irritated her, though she knew they were the "nerves of the day before." As soon as the event—whether it turned out well or ill—took place, the duke would recover his usual calm.

"What'll happen?" he was asking.

"You've always believed victory would be certain and easy."

"When the moment comes, you see the difficulties better. What do you think?"

"There's always some way of winning."

"How?"

"Knowing how to lose is enough."

The duke repeated that he could not stay on in Madrid, and that the day seemed desperately long to him. Finding no better program, they decided to go to Segovia, where the duchess' father was spending the summer. They would lunch with him and return late in the afternoon. She wanted first to make sure that her father was not with "the witch." The duchess might have tolerated this woman, whom she did not know, if it had been merely a question of one of her father's old friends. But many years earlier—she had just been born—this woman had appeared mixed up in the scandal over the mother duchess' death (a poisonous series of tattlings and gossip), and the duke's name was at times bandied about too lightly. Suicide was mentioned, and matters were left officially at that, but people went on talking, and a shadow of doubt had remained in the duchess' conscience, enough so that she could never think of this woman now without repugnance. However, she did not blame her father, and when she analyzed her own leniency of judgment in this difficult matter she would say: "Perhaps I don't accuse him for the sake of convenience."

When the duchess was ready they set out for Segovia. The palace was left locked up, with Rómulo seated on the threshold of the red brick house hidden among the trees on one side of the gates. He had been living there for fifteen years. He glanced over the newspaper at his wife Balbina, who was going busily about her chores. In his imagination, the Rómulo he had glimpsed at the swimming pool and still did not understand was being born, ripening, trying to grow and spread. It was not a completely new vision. He had known that Rómulo when he was about nineteen or twenty. But shortly afterward the image had begun to lose its brave grace, and it ended by losing its very lines and forms. It faded away from him. This Rómulo was surer of life, of himself, but suddenly he would remember the duchess' words—"Rómulo a man?"—and start to waver. He would remember the laugh which followed those words and feel covered with ridicule. He asked his wife:

"What would you say, Balbina, if I asked you what a man is?"

The woman stared at him, trying to guess what was going on in his head. At last she said:

"Don't you know what a man is better than I do?"

But Rómulo was preparing a more difficult question. So difficult he dared not put it. Finally he said:

13

"Would you let His Grace see you naked?"

Feeling flattered, Balbina answered:

"What an idea! Of course not."

"Why?"

"His Grace is a man."

Ah, and Rómulo was not—the duchess had said so. The duchess had laughed—"Rómulo a man?"—because the mere idea of it made her laugh. Rómulo passed his hand over his forehead without understanding. At midday Rómulo could hold out no longer, and he went to look for the duchess' maid and found her sitting at the table in the servants' dining room. Rómulo said to her in a low voice:

"Did you see what happened this morning?"

"You mean you gave Her Grace a letter?"

"Yes, but there was something extraordinary and unusual about it."

"What?"

"Something unbelievable."

The maid offered him a chair.

"That's right. According to regulations it should have been one of the footmen who brought the letter, and not you."

"It isn't that, woman. You know what I mean."

The maid smiled.

"Rómulo, after you've shaved there's a blue shadow left on your face that suits you very nicely."

"Stop talking rubbish. You heard?"

"Heard what?"

"What Her Grace said."

She looked at him, puzzled.

"Her Grace said she was going to Segovia."

Rómulo was beginning to realize that his insistence in front of the uncaring maid was ridiculous.

"All right, all right," he said.

And out he went. He walked slowly back to his house. He thought the incident even more humiliating after having vainly sought its explanation from the maid.

At midafternoon, when Rómulo was in the room which had a window giving onto the street, he heard somebody rap against the pane with a walking stick. He went over to it, but could not see anyone.

"Why don't they ring the bell?"

His wife, Balbina, said:

"It must be Midge."

Out of temper, Rómulo went out to the park.

Near the carriage entrance, was another, much smaller, gate. Outside this stood Midge. In spite of the name, Midge was not a woman, but a man of about forty, so tiny that he scarcely reached to Rómulo's knees. People called him "Midge," short for "midget." He was smartly dressed and had an enormous head with a very dour expression. He was arrogant, and used to refer to himself proudly as "small but smart." He worked in a wax-chandler's shop in the district, and some years before had tried without suc-

cess to enter the palace service. Seeing Rómulo in his
shirtsleeves, he asked:

"Aren't Their Graces at home?"

"No."

"I'm sorry. I came to inform them of something
sensational. *You* can tell them about it, Mr. Rómulo."

"I? About what?"

"Calvo Sotelo has been assassinated."

The name meant nothing to Rómulo. Midge added,
flexing his legs slightly as though to ease his crotch:

"You live in Limbo."

Then, as if it were not worthwhile initiating Rómulo into political life:

"Tell your masters that."

He realized Rómulo did not mean to tell them, and,
in order to show that the palace regulations were not
unknown to him, he added:

"Tell the butler. He'll tell the agent, and the agent
will tell His Grace's secretary."

Then he went strutting off on his short legs. Rómulo
saw him walk over to one of the porches on the other
side of the street, look carefully up and down to make
sure there was nobody about, and draw a swastika on
the door with a piece of chalk. Rómulo went back to
the lodge and said to his wife:

"I can't bear that fellow. He turns my stomach."

"Poor God-forsaken thing!"

"I don't see why you pity him. He's the most self-
satisfied creature I've ever seen in my life."

But Rómulo still felt uneasy, recalling the incident in the swimming pool. He stayed wandering about in the park until nightfall. He could not go to bed until the duke and duchess returned, and it was very late when he heard the car. He opened the gates, dazzled by the headlamps. The light seemed to be coming from the duchess herself, the duchess whom he could not help imagining naked in the car, as she had been in the swimming pool. He was unable to see who else was inside, although he recognized the chauffeur who answered his good night. After locking up, Rómulo retired, and when he had been in bed for an hour the telephone beside him rang. It was the butler speaking, telling him the master would be going out again. Rómulo dressed hastily and went out to open and close the gates. As he was returning, he saw a light in the wing of the palace where the duchess had her rooms. It was very late. He heard a radio in the distance giving the news. Feeling that there was something strange going on in the routine of the house, he went back to his bedroom.

"Something's happening," he said to his wife.

"Yes, I've noticed a lot of commotion, too, as though a baby was being born in the family or an old man dying."

This amused Rómulo, who was trying unsuccessfully to sleep. In the courtyard the agitation continued. Telephones rang frequently. Balbina told him he ought to get up and dress in case they called him, but

Rómulo did not answer. At last the lights began to go out, and eventually the noises died away.

At eight o'clock the following day, Madrid was a battlefield. By ten the struggle seemed to be concentrated in the Cuartel de la Montaña, an agglomeration of military buildings overlooking a hill between the Plaza de España and Rosales, isolated by parks and avenues. At midday, after several assaults which cost hundreds of lives, the people of Madrid managed to capture the hill and suppress the rebels. The whole aspect of the city had changed in the space of a few hours. The strangest things took place quite simply and naturally. The workaday air of Madrid quivered festively with cannon shot. In the courtyard of the Cuartel de la Montaña, more than fifty officers and leaders were found dead after the battle. The Duke of Alcanadre's papers appeared in the pockets of one of them.

Toward the middle of the afternoon, the Hispano car in which the duke had gone out the previous night appeared at the palace gates. There were two bullet holes in the windshield. The car was full of youths with rifles and Republican arm bands. Rómulo stared at them uncomprehendingly. It seemed to him that they could not be "in earnest." "It's just like making a film," he thought.

"Isn't this the master's car?" he asked naïvely.

"The master doesn't exist," said one of the militiamen, stressing *the master*, "and the car's been requisitioned by the Republican militias."

So saying, he pointed to a stamped paper gummed on the windshield. Rómulo asked the men to wait and went into the palace. The duchess was in the hall, peering out through the glass. Rómulo walked along repeating to himself that word—"requisitioned"—which he had heard for the first time in his life. As for the remark about "the master doesn't exist," he did not know what to make of it. Standing before the duchess, who viewed him in silence, he began feeling like "the other Rómulo" again. He repeated the militiaman's words, and the duchess, rather pale, said:

"It's useless to resist. Let them in."

The old butler intervened:

"Before they're let in, Her Grace had better withdraw."

She went slowly toward the elevator. Its sliding doors, fitted between two pillars, concealed it perfectly. Rómulo went out and opened the gates, and the car drove in and pulled up violently at the front door. The militiamen clambered out and went inside. Two of them remained at the door with shouldered rifles. They all had tired eyes and sunburnt faces. There was a hint of danger in their movements, but their way of listening was full of poise and responsibility. The butler assured them that none of the ducal family was at home. The militiamen believed him, and the one who seemed to be the patrol leader said: "That's

19

only natural, they wouldn't be waiting for us." Behind a large glass panel, the servants were beginning to gather, without daring to come out. A militiaman asked the butler:

"Is there anyone here who belongs to any Republican party?"

The butler made a negative gesture. One militiaman ordered the servants to come out, and, when they were all drawn up in a wide semicircle, he said:

"Isn't there at least somebody on the kitchen or garden staff who's joined a trades-union?"

Rómulo was looking at the Hispano, which had three white initials painted on the windshield. He remembered he had some papers and a "card" headed by those very letters. Months before someone had insisted on his joining, and Rómulo had done so to please him, thinking the matter unimportant. He stepped forward and said:

"Me. I'm in a trades-union that has those same initials."

"Very well," said the militiaman. "All the rest of you are to leave the house. You'll keep the keys and be answerable to us that nobody goes in or out of here without your knowledge. Have you any arms?"

"No."

They were going to give him a pistol but demanded first to see his union card, and Rómulo went to fetch it. When he returned, the militiaman handed him the weapon and said to the others:

20

"You've got two hours to leave this building, which from now on belongs to the Republic, that's to say, the people."

The house was searched in summary fashion. The servants were going about weeping and finishing their packing. The militiamen started hunting through the duke's private papers, but it seemed a wearisome and fruitless task. One of them said they were wasting their time, and besides they were not cut out for policemen. As for the duchess, nobody asked after her. The militiamen went down to the *salle d'armes* and took away some belts, halters and other straps, and three pairs of riding boots. Rómulo accompanied them, and standing near the swimming pool he reconstructed in his memory the scene of the previous day. The sunlight no longer streamed through the high windows, but the dark, juicy green of branches was visible. Rómulo listened attentively to the militiamen's questions and replied in a simple, truthful voice. These men, dressed in civilian clothes like anybody else, with rifles slung over their shoulders and bands on their sleeves, gave him no impression of authority whatever. The news that the duke was dead appeared incredible to him, and its improbability lent an unreal tone to everything else. But when they were leaving the *salle d'armes,* and a militiaman who was carrying a foil stuck it into the protective plastron on the dummy, Rómulo thought the man's act showed surprising ease and mastery, and he began to think there might be something true in all this. When the militia-man who was apparently the leader gave him a Republican arm band to wear, with a blue seal stamped on the yellow edging of the national colors, and told him: "Your salary will be paid by the National Requisition Junta," Rómulo admitted to himself that under certain conditions the Duke of Arlanza's house might perhaps come to an end. Rómulo received the keys—the whole bunch of them—from the butler but could not get used to carrying them and having the right to open and shut and manage things without giving an account to anybody. For the time being, the ducal household existed only in the person of the duchess, who remained hidden and was at his mercy. Whenever Rómulo paused to consider this, he saw himself as another person again—as the Rómulo of his youth—and the unheralded change then came about so swiftly that it left him no time to think. It was as though life itself were offering him the picture of that other and now faded Rómulo, losing all the secret laws which made it solemn and dreadful, and turning into a joke.

The militiamen had gone, and Rómulo went back to his lodgings quite late in the afternoon. He put the keys—more than fifty keys with their tabs and numbers—on the table with the pistol. For a long time he stood gazing at them and trying to set his ideas in order. Nearly all the things he had done seemed to have an obscurely dangerous sense.

"I saw all the servants leave without saying a word."

"I went through their baggage like a policeman, and when I found some valuable things in the cook's stuff that I couldn't prove belonged to him, I took them out at the militiamen's request."

"I let the militiamen keep the Hispano."

"I couldn't do anything to prevent it, but I made myself responsible in a way by showing them the Buick and the Chevrolet as well, which were in the garage, and they'll come to fetch them tomorrow."

"I accepted the Republican arm band and the pistol."

When he reached this point, he asked his wife for the arm band, and she told him she had thrown it in the fire, since they had enough troubles already. Rómulo held his peace. He went out into the park again. In the distance, stray shots could be heard through the freshening air, which seemed perfumed by the dusk. The twilight was a festive twilight, too. Rómulo recalled the duchess in the nude. "It's that nakedness that's caused all this confusion," he said to himself, quite convinced. "How? Why? That I shall never know." Rómulo gazed at the empty, silent park, with the clumps of box turning black in the darkness, and the poplars becoming a luminous green instead. He remembered the gala nights—the great celebrations. The park and the house and the very sky over them had seemed then to be made of glass. And now he

23

looked at the deserted park, and the pillars upholding
the gates, and said to himself: "I don't know what else
can happen, after seeing the mistress like I saw her
yesterday, but everybody's in a holiday mood." He
was carrying the keys in his hand and stared at them
abstractedly. "It's war, but what war is it? What kind
of war? And what else is going to happen tonight or
tomorrow?" Rómulo was looking at the avenue of
cypresses. The duke had been killed. In the high
branches the birds were raising the same hubbub they
did every night before they settled down to sleep. Rómulo asked himself anxiously if what he had done—or
not done—was right. He rubbed his hard hand along
his jaw with a rough sound, as though his skin were
made of cardboard. "They've all gone off on their own
affairs. And what about me?" He went back to his
house. Soon afterward, he heard the rap of a stick on
the window again. Balbina said:

"It's Midge."

Rómulo, irritated by this way of knocking, murmured:

"Why doesn't he ring the bell?"

Balbina reminded him that Midge could not reach
the bell with his hand. Rómulo went out. In his pale-
colored hat, Midge looked like a mushroom that had
grown up between the paving stones on the sidewalk.
He showed Rómulo a pistol he was wearing stuck in
his belt:

"Tell Their Graces I'm theirs to command."

24

Without waiting for a reply, he started off down the street. But suddenly he came back and said:

"Their Graces must surely remember a jockey they had about six years ago. His name was Froilan. Tell them I'm his second cousin on my mother's side."

He exhibited the butt of his revolver again, turned aside to spit, and said:

"The Reds are looking for me. If they keep on looking for me, I'll see to it that they find me."

He went away. Rómulo did not understand. "The Reds." And likewise "Calvo Sotelo." The swastika crosses on the doors. The midget being tracked down. Who could really be tracking down a midget? And yet the midget was "protecting Their Graces." Rómulo understood less all the time. He sat down on the threshold of his lodgings. The duchess was on the top floor of the tower. He imagined her naked. He was unable to think of her that day except like this. There were five guest apartments in the tower that had not been used for a long time. That is to say, four, because the ground floor had been shut up since the mother duchess died. Rómulo was looking at the tower. He wanted to do something for the duchess, but the only thing he could do was wait for her orders. It was dark by the time the telephone rang in the lodge. It was the duchess calling him. She seemed as tranquil as ever and asked Rómulo to light the furnace in an old boilerhouse that was no longer used, in order to heat the water in the tower, and to bring her a radio set.

She went on talking lightly, in a perfectly calm frame of mind—nobody would have thought her husband had just died—and ended by telling him to be careful of his actions, because one day he might have to explain them. Although she told him this in a tone of friendly warning, Rómulo felt troubled as he crossed the park, without understanding why those words had sounded to him like a threat.

When he came upstairs with the radio, he found the duchess wandering about and staring at everything with the interested detachment of a person who has just moved into a new house. Rómulo made a conventional remark about "his deepest sympathy for Her Grace in her bereavement." The duchess looked at him as though noticing him for the first time.

"Why tell lies, Rómulo?" she asked, smiling. "You don't feel the duke's death, and that's only natural. So it isn't necessary to say anything."

The duchess was walking about, trying to get used to the atmosphere of these rooms in which she had never lived before. They were spacious and comfortable. There were crystal chandeliers with antique cornucopias in them, and the wall hangings were pale. The bedroom, next to the terrace, was fitted out like a prince's chamber. The duchess did not feel badly off here, but she had heard old stories about the tower, and as the afternoon declined she kept glancing from side to side as though fearful of seeing her dead grandparents' forms materialize in the air. When

Rómulo appeared she felt more at ease. Rómulo stood in front of her, but he avoided looking at her, because behind the duchess, on the wall, there was a huge seascape, with a blue sky and waves breaking on a low shore. The duchess' face was right in front of the water, as on a beach. Or as in the swimming pool. Rómulo presently became aware that the duchess was asking him something. Places that have not been lived in for a long time have an unfamiliar sonority, and Rómulo was slow in grasping what she was saying. The duchess was asking him if the militiamen had told him when they meant to set up a permanent guard. Rómulo replied that it would be next day, but he tried to soothe her by saying that the palace was very large and he would watch out for her safety day and night.

"The Reds sacked the house, I suppose?" she asked.

"No, My Lady. They haven't touched anything."

The duchess looked at him coolly:

"Good fellows, eh?"

Rómulo was about to say yes, but he restrained himself, and instead of nodding he put his head on one side and opened his arms a little. His position seemed to him so forward that he did not know what to say. He was at last on the point of speaking, when the duchess said to him in a voice of friendly reproach:

"I don't want any false situations in my house. Rómulo, you are free to do as you please. You can leave like the others if you want to."

27

Rómulo blurted out:

"I'd rather stay in Her Grace's service."

The duchess felt obliged to warn him that the situation might last for months.

"My Lady, even if it's years, I still mean it."

The duchess was silent and watched him.

"But there's one thing I don't understand. Why did they give the keys to you and not to somebody else?"

Rómulo thought: "Ah, Her Grace would rather they had given them to somebody else, the butler perhaps." But he answered by explaining minutely what had happened. Although the palace servants were forbidden to join trades-unions, Rómulo spoke of his card with such ease and innocence that it disarmed the duchess. She let him talk. Shots could still be heard, some far away and others nearer. The duchess appeared to listen to them in the same mechanical and unconcerned manner. She asked:

"Are there any more surprises, Rómulo?"

She was looking at him again, with that "disinterest" which humiliated Rómulo. "You don't look at a human being like that," he told himself, "only at an animal or a piece of furniture." The duchess was speaking:

"Have you got the pistol with you that the Reds gave you?"

"Yes, My Lady."

The duchess stretched out her hand. Rómulo gave her the pistol, and the duchess laid it on the chair arm.

"Thank you."

After a long silence she picked it up again and handed it back to him.

"Keep it, and think whom you ought to use it on, if you ever have to shoot."

The duchess, smiling broadly—"and her husband just dead!" Rómulo was thinking—took another pistol from the crack between the cushions and the back of the divan and showed it to him in the palm of her hand. It was small, with gold and mother-of-pearl mountings. Seeing that weapon in the duchess' hands, Rómulo knew he was in a false position. They looked like two enemies. He could never have imagined the duchess with a weapon in her hands. He kept looking behind and above the duchess at the huge seascape hanging on the wall, full of fluid blues like the divan cover, like the little rainbows in the prisms of the cornucopias. He said with firmness:

"Perhaps I've done something foolish, but all I know is how to tend the park. Does My Lady think it's not a good thing to belong to a union?"

"Good or bad, it's expressly forbidden in this household."

"Excuse me, My Lady, but Father Lucas, who used to come to the servants' mass, spoke to us about the advantage of belonging to a union."

The duchess realized that Rómulo had not listened to Father Lucas, or had listened with only half an ear as she herself usually did:

"But Father Lucas was speaking about the Catholic trades-union."

"Excuse me, My Lady, but I remember quite well it was the Free Trades-Union."

"Of course, of course."

The fact that Catholic unions were called free unions was something Rómulo could never comprehend. The duchess rose, saying:

"All right, never mind. Thank you for your loyalty, Rómulo."

Rómulo had noticed the lighted lamps and that one of the windows was open. The light could be seen from the park, and if the militiamen returned they would ask who lived there, and difficult explanations would have to be made. Rómulo warned the duchess:

"It's dark by now, My Lady, and the lights will give you away to people looking from outside."

"Very well, close the window and go. I'll call you if I need you."

The gardener closed not only that window but all the others as well, and bowed and went into the elevator.

Left to herself, the duchess went to the desk, picked up a small book bound in white leather, and began writing composedly:

"The duke is alive, as I've heard over the telephone. Poor Rómulo, seeing me so cheerful, must think I'm a heartless woman.

"I'm not worried about what may have happened to

Father. Yesterday we decided that if our people didn't win immediately he'd go and take refuge in one of the embassies. Besides, what I heard by telephone, vague as it was, is enough to set my mind at rest. It was the Baron of C.'s voice that spoke to me, though he naturally didn't give his name. He knows how to swim and hold onto his clothes. I was imprudent enough to ask too eagerly after Estéban, the Marquis of R., the handsome Satan. They're friends, and Estéban will soon find out that I'm anxious about him. That really is. . . ." But she did not want to write too much, for fear the notes might fall into somebody's hands one day.

"I'm not in any danger. These men of the people really believe it's noble to respect women, and I feel sure that if they find me they won't do me any harm. Besides, beauty disarms the people—let me say it without modesty. I'm only hiding to avoid difficulties —arrests, questioning—and because, in a week's time, our side will either have won or be definitely lost. My side are the Monarchists; I don't want to be mixed up with certain other folk. I really don't know how they can bring Alfonso XIII to me here, but perhaps he'll come riding in on a cloud and descend gently onto the throne to the strains of the Royal March.

"Rómulo's the one who believes I'm in danger. Or perhaps he doesn't believe it, and is just speculating to give himself airs after the scene in the swimming pool. I realize that was a crazy thing to do. I realize

31

it now, after seeing how providence—my confessor would scold me for saying providence instead of God —has punished me by putting me at the mercy of a gardener whom I may have humiliated too much. Sometimes I think there's a fatal set of compensations in life, managed by a stern, indifferent judge. I must verify the information about Father's condition."

Meanwhile the elevator had reached the bottom and halted with a soft thud. Rómulo came out of it and crossed the park, feeling vaguely sad in those lonely spaces, full of shadows, that had once been friendly and were now disquieting, and entered his house. His wife was crying. After eating supper they went to bed. Rómulo, recalling the interview with the duchess, thought he had behaved well. She had wanted him to talk to her, and perhaps he had not talked enough, but just the same the duchess had appeared to be forcing him into silence with her indifference, her careless smile. In any case it was difficult to talk facing that picture on the wall, so full—he did not know why— of allusions to feminine nakedness. In spite of it all, Rómulo lay smiling. His smile began to disappear little by little. Balbina kept on sobbing and repeating: "Her poor Grace the duchess, so young and beautiful, and she's lost everything in life!" Rómulo could not stand the pleasure and voluptuousness hidden behind those words. He got up and went out of the door. He walked over to have a look at the furnaces that heated the tower water, threw on some more coal, and returned to his house. The furnaces were in a separate place in the park, behind the washhouses. Once again the park seemed to him forlorn and silent. The lights had not been turned on—why should they be? The garage doors were open, showing like an accusation the place where the Hispano had been.

As he went homeward, he heard the telephone ringing in the tower of the palace. "If those militiamen come back," he thought, "and hear that bell, it's going to be difficult to explain it." But after a short while no further noises came from the tower.

He could not sleep. Toward midnight, after great doubts, he decided to disconnect the telephone. He went out in his undervest and slippers—a liberty he would never have allowed himself to take if the master had been in the house—and, while he was at it, he thought: "This isolates Her Grace; it shuts her in more and deprives her of the comfort of talking to friends or maybe a relation; but I can't help doing it if I want to guard her life." Once it was done he went back home, and the idea that the duchess was cut off from everybody gratified him. Distant gunfire could still be heard. "War's war."

Balbina was not asleep either, and she spent the time reminding him of all the most notable episodes in the duke's life. Rómulo had to put up with her lamentations. Whenever he grew drowsy, she would notice and cry louder to keep him awake. At last Rómulo gave up trying to sleep and applied himself

33

to making sure there was no light in the tower. He was thinking about the duchess. "Perhaps when she's alone she weeps like my wife, but in front of me she smiles because I mustn't come into the world of her feelings." This made him feel a certain tenderness coupled with some disappointment. He sat down by the door and remained there for long hours.

But the duchess was not weeping. She was awake in bed, leafing through a book. It was the third she had taken from the shelves, and after reading a couple of pages she closed it and went to get another.

She could not read. She kept remembering the scene in the swimming pool with Rómulo. Except for recent events—the uprising, the defeat—she would never have recalled the incident. Being forced to see Rómulo often now, and show gratitude for a loyalty that appeared doubtful to her where once it had been certain and assured, she became immersed in moral considerations and presently muttered without realizing she was speaking:

"It was rash of me."

To take her mind off it, she started reading again. But it was not long before she fell asleep. She awoke in the middle of the night, thinking she had heard something. The little bedside lamp, no brighter than a firefly, was still burning but shone only as far as the edge of the bed. The shadows beyond seemed to crowd round and hem her in. With sudden decision, she jumped out of bed and went into the adjoining room. On the divan a man was sitting with his back to her. She gave a cry, and the man turned round. It was the duke, her husband.

"My dear, what a fright you gave me!"

He rose and kissed her.

"Forgive me," he said, "I didn't want to wake you."

She thought his eyes looked feverish, as though harassed by the stormy events of that July day. There was a lack of self-knowledge about him which the duchess felt she had never seen before. She found him suddenly hardened, more mature. But somewhat ghostly. His words had an inner echo, as though coming from immense and uninhabited spaces.

"Are you all right?" she asked him.

"So far, yes."

The duke spoke of what had happened in the Cuartel de la Montaña, but the duchess did not appear to be listening. In his expression, in his tone of voice, she was looking for those things he did not say although he wanted to, for in the tension produced by events he had not been able to think about them yet. "He's empty," she told herself, "and the air of his emptiness is frozen." They sat near the terrace door. She asked, as though it were an assertion:

"There's no hope, is there?"

The duke thought the same, but he could not bear to hear anyone else say it.

"You mustn't talk like that. You see, there's too

much involved. If the worst comes to the worst, we can't lose. But it's hard, of course. People get killed."

Listening to him speak, she thought: "There are little will-o'-the-wisps in his inner void, like the ones in old cemeteries." The duke was mentioning names. Three of her relatives and two of his had died. The duchess would never have believed these people capable of dying heroically. The duke went on talking. The Marquis of R., Estéban, had managed to escape, like himself, a little before the Cuartel de la Montaña was captured by the Republicans. Speaking of Estéban, the duke seemed more resolute, and the duchess more attentive to his words. Estéban had had the idea of changing coats with a dead civilian, and he had done likewise with an officer, because he was in uniform. In the pockets were identity papers. Later, at Estéban's house . . . that is to say, at a "stamping ground" of his . . . but the duchess did not understand this term, and her husband told her it meant a more or less clandestine place for Don Juanish adventures. The duchess smiled. There Estéban had given him civilian clothes, but the duke had kept the papers of the dead officer, Lieutenant Martinez Hungria. With his new personality he felt safe for the moment, since it was not likely the militiamen knew this officer, but there was some danger. . . .

The duchess interrupted him:

"Are you living there?"

"Where?"

"At the . . . 'stamping ground'?"

"Ah," thought the duke, "the idea of the 'stamping ground' has stuck in her imagination." And aloud he added:

"Yes, for the time being. It's an apartment rented under an assumed name. Nobody in the house knows that Estéban is the Marquis of R."

"What does Estéban say?"

"His position is quite different. He's heavily responsible."

The duchess did not understand. She watched the will-o'-the-wisps trembling in the duke's nervous silences. Weren't they all equally responsible? Or perhaps her husband had not fought?

"That's just it," he said. "I fought. I'm a soldier. But I'm only a soldier, nothing more. That is to say, outside of military action I'm incapable of killing anybody. Whereas Estéban. . . . But why talk about it? We've been beaten in Madrid, even if the movement finally wins. For the present we're beaten here, and we should have realized it and surrendered."

The duchess noticed that between her husband's looks and his words were strange lulls, and in them a certain incongruence.

"Surrender? Isn't that dangerous?"

"It gets worse with every hour we let go by. All

because of Estéban and others like him. At the present moment," he added thoughtfully, "you may be right; perhaps it's suicide."

They fell silent. The duke added:

"Estéban killed several men in cold blood, just like that. They were the first shots fired in Madrid. Those men had refused to join the uprising, and the captain of their company disarmed them and sent them to the lockup. When Estéban arrived, he made them come out and killed them one by one, shooting them through the chest. He's done hundreds of other awful things. I'm no sentimentalist, but all that's quite unnecessary and makes it impossible for us to demand the rights of prisoners of war."

She asked him what he had done at the Cuartel de la Montaña. The duke, who was an auxiliary officer in the artillery, felt rather surprised at his own voice as he said:

"I was in command of a battery that fired about a hundred rounds. The planes dismantled three of my guns in the first half hour. I did what I could. I'd do the same thing all over again, because I believe it's my duty. But I don't understand Estéban. He says the people are right, and we've got to trounce their rightness out of them with bullets. He's crazy."

"Where is Estéban?"

"Down below, keeping watch."

"Isn't it dangerous for the two of you to go about together?"

After a pause, the duke shrugged. The duchess looked at him uncomprehendingly:

"At least when you come to see me, come by yourself. If you come with him, we'll all three be killed some day."

The duke spoke like an automaton:

"My new identity won't do for very long, because the government's called up all the officers of the Madrid garrison by radio. I'm Lieutenant Martinez Hungria. If I show up, somebody might recognize me, and if I don't, I'm a deserter."

"They'll shoot you if they recognize you."

The duke lighted a second cigarette and jerked his hand in the air to put out the match. He did all this with a certain arrogance.

"Probably."

He saw that his wife's eyes had lost the wan opaqueness that gave them a pitying expression. He said he was tired, walked over to the bed, and dropped down onto it. He took a deep breath and, as he let it out again, remarked in a sinking voice:

"Years have passed since yesterday!"

He had caught a book under him. He pulled it out and read the title: *Religious Symbolism of Colors in the Middle Ages.* He flung it to one side and said:

"Centuries ago you could do certain things, but nowadays it's impossible to see them done without protesting."

She did not reply. The duke added:

"Killing as they're killing today is stupid. And we started it. The mob's learning the lesson. If they learn it too well, can we wonder?"

The duchess still remained silent, and he asked her:

"Haven't you anything to eat?"

She too felt hungry, but there was nothing in the tower. The duke went down to the pantry and the cellar. He returned with olives, caviar, and an enormous hunk of roast beef. He was also carrying a bottle of champagne chilled by the cold cellar. The duke opened the bottle, muffling the pop of the cork, and asked after Rómulo. She explained what had happened. Contrary to what she had expected, the duke spoke well of the gardener. The duchess said to herself: "He'd speak well of the whole lot of them. He's afraid of his own feelings. Blood and hate weary him." They both stopped talking. Filling a glass, the duke said.

"Say something to me, my dear. Silence makes me nervous."

"Just now," she said, "you ought to have only one idea on your mind: how to avoid danger, and escape. Perhaps if we could hold out for a few months. . . ."

The duke arched his eyebrows:

"A few weeks, I'd say," and the glass shook in his fingers.

He took another sip and added:

40

"Estéban says a few days."

She ventured a joke about the anguish of the three of them:

"I think our calculations are influenced by how safe each of us feels."

The duke took the idea from her lips:

"I thought of that, too. You believe victory will take a few months, because you think you'll be able to wait here in hiding for a few months. As I can hold out only a few weeks, I hope for victory sooner. And Estéban says a few days. He's an optimist. In his case, I'd say a few hours."

The duke laughed, and that laugh was the first thing the duchess liked about him. The duke lit another cigarette, smoked more than half of it in silence, and then began talking again, puffing the smoke out slowly between his words:

"If we'd won, we'd be patriots, Christian heroes, et cetera, et cetera. The ones who did the same thing in Valladolid are lucky. But we haven't won in Madrid, and so what are we? What are we, ten hours later?"

"Don't drink any more," the duchess told him.

"Why? Do you think I'm drunk?"

"If you have to leave here before dawn, it's better not to drink much."

She was afraid of her husband's fear. The duke sat down on the divan with sudden touchiness. "She doesn't want me to drink too much," he thought, "because then I mightn't be able to leave, and the prospect of my staying annoys her."

"Don't worry. I intend to go as soon as I've smoked this cigarette."

Expecting the duchess to grow tender and remonstrate lovingly with him, he heard her say instead:

"That'll be best. And next time, if you want to stay here longer, don't come with Estéban."

"That's true," he said convinced. "You're always right about practical things."

He went over to her, kissed her on the neck, and said:

"We're captives. His Excellency, the Captive of Alcanadre; His Excellency, the Marquis of R.; Captives, with the executioner following us from pillar to post. Sometimes I even fancy I can see him, and whenever I stop and look back I seem to hear him saying: 'Hallo!' "

His nostrils were quivering.

"What perfume have you got on?"

"None."

The duke came nearer and said confidentially:

"Do you know what that swine Estéban said to me?"

"What?"

"He told me if I stayed here too long it would whet his appetite."

The duchess thought: "That good-looking Satan is pushing his impudence too far with him." The duke put his arms round her. She clasped him gently in return, pressing against him from knee to shoulder. She lifted her face for a kiss, but at that moment the duke glanced over her shoulder at his wristwatch, with a vexed, absent-minded gesture, and she saw this gesture in the mirror. Feeling she had mistaken her "cue," she let go of him, rather offended. She walked away into the next room, and her husband followed her. She sat down on the divan. She had picked up a book from the bed as she passed, and she opened it at random. Her glance fell on some lines about "the craze for green, which may be either mystic or carnal madness." The duke was asking her:

"Are you offended because of what I told you about Estéban?"

She shook her head and rose:

"It's late."

She did not really know what time it was, and spoke in such a neutral voice that the duke, had he wished, could have noticed something like satisfaction in it. She was glad it was late. The duke dropped into a chair:

"Don't you know that this may be my last visit?" he asked, using an argument he would have preferred to avoid.

"Yes. I do know it."

They both fell silent again. In the duke's inner void, things resembling birds of prey were softly flying.

"Have *I* offended you, then?"

The duchess shook her head without conviction and

43

without wanting to convince him. As she did not speak, the duke also retired into silence. Afterward he got up and said he would like to take a bath. "The water won't be clean all night," she said, reminding him that the pipes in that part of the palace had not been used for a long time. The duke insisted. "I'm used to that trick," thought the duchess. "The duke has a rather comic confidence in his bare body." She added:

"If you'd like to wait. . . ."

The duke said nothing, and, when he seemed about ready to leave, she went to the bathroom and remarked from the doorway:

"Perhaps it can be fixed."

The hot water came out dirty, but it soon began to lose color. Seeing that the whole matter would be solved in five minutes, the duke connected the duchess' last warning—"it won't be clean all night"—with the previous one about the time and shut himself up in his reserve again. She wanted to get rid of him. The duchess stood up, suitably sorry, and went into the bedroom. She stood there looking at a picture. It was a last-century French engraving, at which she could not glance without shuddering. It showed some people leaving a ball, and, among the top hats, fur coats, smiles, and bouquets, a gruesome guest (a skeleton dressed up as a woman) was arching its waist coquettishly and seeming to listen to some madrigal with the dry holes in its cranium. The duchess tried to take this picture down, but the frame was heavy, and, besides, it was hanging from a wire that reached up to the cornice. When the duke emerged from the bathroom with a towel wrapped round his waist, she hastily told him to take the picture outside "before leaving." The duke looked at her without knowing what to think, went over to the picture, and saw a sentence printed in big letters below the engraving: "*Les charmes de l'horreur n'enivrent que les forts.*" She thought: "They make strong people drunk, people like Estéban." The duke was trying to unhitch the picture, standing on a chair. She looked at him, almost naked, and repeated to herself: "As usual, he's got a childish confidence in his body." But if these athletic exhibitions were by way of making things easier, they never appeared so to the duchess, and in this lack of harmony lay a discouraging void. Getting into bed, she explained:

"The idea of that skeleton having any youthful attractions irritates and alarms me. How could it have?"

The duke carried the picture out to the anteroom and left it leaning with its back against the wall. The duchess entreated:

"Don't leave it there. That's worse."

The duke went down the dark stairs with it and took it to the floor below, the fourth floor. Presently he returned, but the duchess was not yet satisfied.

"Now I have the mark that picture made on the

wall right opposite my bed. Can't you cover it up with something?"

The duke, slightly pale, was getting impatient.

"Tell me what you want done."

"Put another picture there, but don't take it out of the anteroom. Fetch it from the library."

He protested:

"You want to make me dress and go all the way over there, turning on lights and drawing attention to us."

The duchess watched him come to the bed, lift up the sheet. It was a huge double bed, but she made a gesture of annoyance.

"If I'm in your way. . . ." he said, hesitating.

"No, but it's too hot."

She went to a cupboard and fetched a fresh sheet, which she kept for herself, leaving the other one entirely to him. She explained that with two sheets, and avoiding touching each other, they would both be fairly cool, but the duke pushed her down and overcame her by force. She had been like a passive slave, taking nothing of the feast. His nerves once eased, the duke lay breathing deeply and slowly. In a tone halfway between depression and sarcasm, he remarked:

"I hope you aren't going to make me apologize."

She lay silent, as though in revenge. But she had been overcome morally too. Seeing she made no reply, the duke started a monologue. The duchess noticed how the empty frozen reaches from which his

46

words came were filling, little by little, with living shapes and warm breezes.

"Thirty-two's not much of an age, is it? I've got you here beside me, and that's all I have got. (The duchess was saying to herself: "He needs confidences, as usual, after love.") I've spent the whole day out in the blazing sun with a madman. (The duchess asked: "Estéban?") Yes, with a madman who puts a crazy coherency into his actions. What's to be done with him? Even if they kill him, I think he'd only take it as another joke. Can you imagine it? I've a feeling he's enjoying all this. Don't think I'm talking just for the sake of talking. You won't believe what I'm going to tell you, and I wouldn't have believed it myself unless I'd seen it. Estéban was speaking to the leader of an armed patrol, and he began talking badly about himself in the third person. He told him the Marquis of R. ought to be hanged and said this marquis was one of the chief culprits. Isn't that a silly, crazy thing to do? Luckily the worker didn't recognize the name, and I don't think it stuck in his memory, either, for him to connect with Estéban's idiotic face, but can you imagine it? He did these things with frightful calm. (The duchess was thinking: "He admires Estéban. He admires him and is maybe afraid of him.") *I* don't mind dying either . . . you understand? It's bound to happen some day, and you're too close to things to be able to stop and think about them. It can't be so very terrible. Anyway, before you die you're still alive. The same as now. And after you're dead, what are the odds?"

He sat up in bed. He stared at his wife, trying to read her expression. She looked calm and friendly, saying, "We shouldn't talk about these things. What's the use? Somewhere Death's talking about you and me." She thought of the French engraving. "Let him talk, and do his job when and how and where he has to. That's his business and not ours." After a pause, she asked him why he had not covered the mark left by the picture he had taken down with another of the same size. Annoyed, the duke rose with ill-humored negligence and disappeared down the tower stairs. When he returned and hung up the new picture, she showed a childish gratitude. The night became idyllic, its menacing circumstances merely adding a further attraction. The sound of the words they lazily exchanged moved in those regions, behind reality, where echoes move.

Dawn was approaching slowly. Just before the first light, the duke suddenly remembered Estéban.

"We've forgotten about him waiting down there."

"Let him wait," she said.

"No. You don't know what he's like. He's capable of coming up here."

Talking of Estéban, they parted on the stairs. The "devil's" name lingered on her lips and on his with the same fondness. Before going, the duke enjoined her to treat Rómulo kindly.

CHAPTER
T W O

IN THE COOLNESS OF EARLY MORNING, RÓMULO took the pruning shears and started trimming some of the clumps of box near the old coach house. The methodical snipping noise was like a seal of normalcy on the quietude of the park. But the Reds might return at any moment. If their curiosity became dangerous for the duchess, he was prepared to go to any lengths, but he did not see how his willingness to risk everything was going to be of much real use to her. He thought of her in the swimming pool, floating in the downy foam; he remembered her feet, as small and pulpy as twin fruits, and wondered: "Why did she want to stay on top of the water except to let me see her?" He warned his wife:

"Get used to the idea that Her Grace is supposed to be dead from now on, the same as her husband, and if they ever make you talk about them you'd better say something against them."

She protested:

"With His Grace the duke lying under a yard of holy earth, you want me to start talking badly about him?"

Rómulo felt he needed to see the duchess but he dared not go until she called him, or at least until later in the morning when there would be less risk of finding her in bed. Toward nine o'clock, the same militiamen arrived as on the previous day, accompanied by four others whom Rómulo had not seen before and who did not look at all military or warlike, although they carried rifles. They seemed quite elderly. They had brought a Republican flag to hoist on the house. The chief of the patrol that had requisitioned the house the day before said, pointing to the new militiamen: "These comrades are going to be the permanent guard here."

The first thing they wanted to do was to put up the flag. Someone spoke of hanging it in the fifth-floor window of the tower—where the duchess was—but Rómulo told them the window was condemned and could not be reached from the inside. This lie, which could easily have been exposed, he thought, made him guilty toward the men. At the same time he suggested hoisting the flag on top of the lodge, so that it would float jauntily above the gates overlooking the street. The flag was accordingly set up there, on Rómulo's own house, and began fluttering in the breeze. The young militiamen, who were not staying at the palace, got the two other cars out of the garage and took them away. Of the older militiamen, one remained on guard at the gate, and the others repaired to the chauffeur's lodgings over the garage. Rómulo noticed with some bewilderment that they made no attempt to settle in the palace rooms. When everything had been arranged, Rómulo went cautiously to visit the duchess.

He found her more composed than ever. She showed no concern over either the flag or the posting of the guard, which she told him she had seen from a half-opened window. Glancing about him, Rómulo suddenly caught sight of an ash tray full of cigarette ends on one of the tables. This ash tray had not been there last night. And the duchess did not smoke. There were secret staircases in the palace, which Rómulo knew about, and a man must have come in that way. He felt deceived.

"Be careful, My Lady," he warned. "The militiamen are armed, and there's a sentry at the front gate from now on."

The duchess assented mechanically. She moved about, once or twice pulling a window ajar and letting a beam of yellow sunlight into the gloom. Since noticing the ash tray, Rómulo wanted to show a secret liking for the Reds:

"Those militiamen," he said, "seem a pleasant sort of folk."

51

The duchess did not hear him. Rómulo added some further words that sounded more challenging:

"They say the government's winning the war everywhere."

The duchess asked how many militiamen there were in the guard and what they were like. She asked as though inquiring about a private guard placed there for her own protection, and while he answered Rómulo was watching the duchess' head and shoulders against the seascape in the picture and seeing her as if she were floating in the water.

"There are four of them. I think I more or less know three. The one they call Ruiz is too talkative. I I think maybe he hasn't any family, and with My Lady's permission he's rather like those gypsies that roam about the country. There's another militiaman who talks about shooting all the enemies of the Republic. This one talks even more than Ruiz and makes me think of somebody wanting to puff himself up with his own words. The third seems bored; he hardly ever speaks. When they ask him things, he gives jumbled answers without saying yes or no. I believe he's the dangerous one, My Lady. We'll have to be careful of him. The one who's on sentry duty now I haven't been able to get a close look at yet."

Hearing him, the duchess realized that Rómulo possessed shrewd qualities which might be very useful to her some day.

52

"All right," said the duchess. "Why isn't the telephone working?"

Rómulo told her he had disconnected it. The duchess seemed to take fright:

"Who ordered you to? Don't you see you're leaving me cut off, isolated, a real prisoner?"

Rómulo realized that this was precisely what he had wanted to do.

"I thought they might listen to My Lady at the exchange and notify the police."

The duchess was getting angry:

"Any danger I may be in is my own affair, and all you have to do is obey orders."

Rómulo said nothing, but he looked her in the face. The duchess went on:

"I want the telephone right now."

"That's impossible, My Lady."

She was irritated, and her suppressed wrath puzzled Rómulo.

"Excuse me, My Lady. I mean, just now it isn't easy. I'll have to wait for the right moment to connect it again without the men on guard seeing me."

Rómulo begged her to keep the windows always shut and the curtains drawn, so that when she was called on the telephone the bell would not be heard from the park. He left her and came downstairs rather depressed. When he saw the sentry strolling up and down outside in the most unmilitary fashion, he realized that these men could signify no real danger, and that the duchess was perhaps right. He went over to the garage. The three militiamen were still examining the chauffeur's house and joking over every little find. They treated Rómulo with complete confidence. Rómulo had a peasant's skill in making others talk and judging what they meant to conceal by what they said, but his tricks proved unnecessary, since most of the militiamen were loquacious. The gardener noticed they regarded him as a being of another species, not exactly superior or inferior but different and rather funny. The taciturn militiaman was very busy mending a heap of military straps, but occasionally he raised his head and asked a question.

"Are we going to spend the whole summer in this palace?"

López called this militiaman Cartridge. The first time Rómulo heard the name he realized how well it suited him. He was thin and small, and the way his head was joined to his neck and shoulders was somehow reminiscent of a rifle cartridge, though Rómulo could not have told precisely why. This militiaman raised his head and asked Rómulo:

"And what about you? What did you work at here? What was your job in the duke's household?"

"Gardener."

"Was that the lowest job?"

Rómulo smiled.

"I don't know. Anyway, it seemed to me better than

54

working in the kitchen, or getting dressed up to the hilt every day like the footmen."

Hearing him speak, López placed him by his accent: "You're from Cordova."

"Not from the capital; from the province, though."

Imitating his accent, López said:

"Frum a middlin'-zized farrm beyan' Buhalance, two leagues this zide o' Cabra."

"Are you from there, too?" asked Rómulo.

"No," intervened Ruiz. "But those Madrid folk come from everywhere and nowhere."

Rómulo was going off to connect the telephone again, when the militiamen said they wanted to see the inside of the palace. Rómulo's misgivings stirred sharply as they all went toward the front door.

"Was the duchess young and pretty?" asked López.

Rómulo merely smiled.

"In olden times," added the militiaman, "duchesses used to sleep with their gardeners."

Rómulo turned pale, seeing the duchess naked in his imagination, and covered his emotion by opening the door. Cartridge added:

"Thanks to the gardeners and other servants, the dukes' race has been kept fairly healthy."

They all laughed again. Rómulo pretended not to be listening.

"Come on in."

He was thinking about the duchess. He was worried, and not only because of the militiamen's curiosity.

Perhaps she needed the telephone to talk to the person who had smoked those cigarettes last night. Both objects—the ash tray and the telephone—had come to have the same meaning for Rómulo, and by this time he could not think of the duchess without their obtruding on his memory. But the militiamen were talking. He realized they used the familiar "thou" in speaking to him, whereas he addressed them more formally as "you." Ruiz was absorbed in the riches of the house. Each of them made different remarks. Ruiz kept repeating:

"There's real grandeur in all this, but it's due to the painters, sculptors, and architects, who were men of the people."

López wanted to price everything.

"How much would those pictures be worth if they were put on the market?"

But the three were agreed in not understanding how the duke, with all those possessions, had wanted even more, and risen in rebellion. The taciturn militiaman smiled and sometimes slid his hand voluptuously over the tapestries on the walls. Ruiz noticed that Rómulo was looking solemn and rather stiff, his movements careful and his expression hard. He clapped him on the back and said: "What's the matter? You look stunned. You needn't think we're going to steal any of this from you."

López also glanced at him humorously. "You look like one of the kings in a pack of cards," he said.

The three of them laughed. They went over the whole house except the tower, to which the entrance through the lift was concealed, while the first and second floor entrances were covered with hangings, and that of the third floor was in a dark corner which aroused no interest. Even so, Cartridge wanted to poke his nose into it, but Rómulo stood with seeming casualness in front of the door to the stairs, his hand in his pocket with the pistol in it. Then, seeing they went no further, he made a great effort to appear composed, because he feared the taciturn man's shrewd little eyes had noticed. They went on down. Rómulo had not yet connected the telephone, and he was glad of this, since it meant one less risk among the possible incidents of the visit.

To forestall any feeling of surprise, Rómulo prudently notified the militiamen as they were leaving that he would make a complete inspection of the palace every day to prevent fire hazards, and also because, as the house was so big, he was afraid some fugitive might get in secretly at night and hide there. "If that happened," he said smiling, "you'd hold me responsible, and rightly." Ruiz put a hand on his shoulder. He enjoyed repeating this proof of familiarity.

"As far as we're concerned, you can rest easy. You're a man of the people, one of our own kind."

Rómulo returned to his living quarters and then went to connect the telephone. The fact that he was tricking the militiamen and sharing the duchess' secrecy gave him an almost physical pleasure. He came away with the feeling that everything was in order. He noticed that the top windows of the tower were closed and thought with a certain tenderness that the duchess had obeyed him. On re-entering his house he was met by his wife, who began telling him all about the life and wondrous doings of the sentry, about the dangerous operation this man had had two years ago, and other enthralling details. Rómulo kept thinking that the duchess had a "secret life" and how inaccessible this life was to him. And he added, half inquisitive and half offended: "Who can that mysterious visitor be?" Quite late—night was falling—the telephone in the lodge rang, softly, for Rómulo had muffled the bell by tying a handkerchief round it. It was the duchess summoning him. Rómulo went up and found her just the same as she had been that morning, with her usual happy expression. As soon as she saw him she began giving him orders:

"Bring one of the small refrigerators from the kitchen. I'm sure you can manage it without being seen. The men on guard all seem to be over on the other side of the park."

Rómulo kept looking at the half-open window, and the duchess added:

"Shut it if you like."

When Rómulo had done so, she switched on the light. Rómulo left to carry out the duchess' orders and went to the kitchens. To move the icebox, he had to roll it along on two iron cylinders. He managed to get it into the elevator. Once he was back on the fifth floor of the tower, he wiped off his sweat, telling himself: "I'm going to speak to her ladyship about that ash tray." But she came over to him and, pointing to the keys that dangled from his belt, gave him fresh orders:

"That's the key to the cellar. Go down and fetch some bottles of champagne. There's a metal basket that'll hold six."

Rómulo was thinking: "At night they have orgies here, in spite of the duke's being dead." He went down to the cellar with his slow calm gait. Rómulo always walked in real peasant fashion, without haste or hesitation. His inner moods, his joy or sorrow, never influenced the movements of his body, which were reposefully dignified. He went down a flight of stairs, then down some cement steps. The vault was like the crypt of a monastery, with Romanesque columns. Iron shelves between the columns contained thousands of bottles lying on their sides and wrapped in straw casing. He found the lights on, and this puzzled him. While looking for the metal basket, he thought he heard a noise at the other end of the cellar. He listened, holding his breath. "It must be rats," he told himself. But he still felt doubtful and went over to have a look. In one corner he found Midge. At first he thought it was an animal, because he only saw the shaggy head moving about close to the floor, but then beneath the head he saw the pistol, aimed at him. The midget combined threat and entreaty as he said:

"Don't throw me out. If you throw me out, I won't be answerable for what I do."

He put the pistol away and went on speaking:

"The Reds are killing people, and I've gone into hiding here. Don't throw me out."

Rómulo looked at him without answering. He was worried that Midge had got in here secretly, unknown to him, while he was in charge of the park entrances. Midge seemed perturbed, and his arrogance was shaky and intermittent:

"Don't throw me out. I'm here in Their Graces' service. Even supposing you're a Red, which I don't expect of a man like you. . . ."

Rómulo asked:

"How long have you been here?"

"For the last eight hours."

"How did you get in?"

"By the tradesmen's entrance on the Calle de Santa Genoveva."

"That gate was locked. Did you break the lock?"

Midge placed his hand on the butt of the pistol again and avoided answering:

"The Reds are after me," he said at last, by way of excuse.

"After you?"

"Yes. They know I was going around chalking

60

swastikas on the doors of houses where Republicans are living."

Rómulo felt like laughing.

"I don't think they'd kill you for that. At most, they'd give you a good beating."

Midge turned pale with indignation. Rómulo realized there was room for a giant's rage and indignation in that tiny body. The dwarf said:

"Do you think I'm the sort of man to take a beating lying down?"

Rómulo was putting six bottles into a basket and getting ready to leave.

"Can I stay here?" Midge asked.

"I don't know, yet."

Seeing the bottles of champagne and hearing these words, the midget thought the duke and duchess must be in the palace. Rómulo was taking them those bottles—they could only be for them—and perhaps he was going to ask for orders concerning him. But Rómulo inquired again:

"Did you break the lock?"

The dwarf drew back, and his face contracted in a queer way. He bared his teeth like a dog.

"Yes. What if I did?"

Rómulo looked at him without comprehending his reactions:

"Nothing," he said.

Rómulo made sure the cellar had no direct outward vents and that the light could not be seen from outside;

then, feeling reassured, he showed the dwarf a toilet and a faucet in a small dark passageway beyond and told him not to leave here and not to turn on the lights more than necessary. Abruptly, Midge said to him:

"It would be better if you didn't say anything to Their Graces."

"Why?"

"Well, I'm in their service, and you might even say I'm risking my life for them. But I'm not sure they'd understand."

"Have you ever spoken to Their Graces?"

"No, I haven't, no. Never. I've only seen them from a distance."

After a pause, he added:

"Let me just stay here till our side enters Madrid. Why should Their Graces have to know? Let's keep the matter as something between you and me."

Rómulo went over to him, and Midge drew back with the same alarmed expression. Rómulo was thinking: "If I take another step, he'll bare his teeth at me again." He stretched out his hand and suggested:

"Give me that pistol, and I promise I won't say anything to anyone."

Midge gave him the pistol. When he was left weaponless, the dwarf seemed to change color. His skin became greenish gray. He took out half a cigar, lit it, and then remarked:

"My life is in your hands."

Rómulo warned him:

"That passage where the lavatory is leads to the storerooms. The doors are locked, the way the tradesmen's entrance on the Calle de Santa Genoveva was locked. If you break that lock. . . ."

"Don't worry."

Then Midge reminded him that jockeys were higher up on household staffs than gardeners, and that he was Froilan the jockey's second cousin. Rómulo put away Midge's pistol and said to him:

"They call you Midge . . . ?"

"The Reds. The district Reds. But their doors are marked, and a day of reckoning will come for all of them."

Rómulo told Midge that he would bring him something to eat from time to time and then left. He took the champagne up to the duchess. He was going to speak to her about the midget, but the subject seemed to him unworthy of her. "Although"—he thought— "if I don't tell her, I'll have to put Midge out of the house, because I can't keep anybody here without her permission." He had to fetch up cold meat, too, canned food, and bottles of liqueur and table wine. In the end, Rómulo was so tired and so harried that he could not nerve himself to confront the mystery of the ash tray. The duchess finished putting the bottles into the icebox and looked at Rómulo.

"If I need you, I'll call."

Rómulo left without venturing to form an opinon of what he had seen. The duchess, a two days' widow, receiving somebody at night. He recalled the glance of haughty confidence with which she had said: "If I need you, I'll call." That glance had seemed to reach him from a surface of shifting waters. And it was as though she kept within herself some remnants of the vivid daylight that was dying away over the tiled roofs of the Calle de Segovia. He was leaving the duchess naked—he thought—awaiting the night.

Meanwhile, the duchess was writing in her diary:

"The duke is coming again tonight. With his dead eyes and living hands. Danger seems only to produce a kind of indifference in him, a withdrawal from himself.

"Rómulo's animal melancholy makes me wonder. He's got that *salle d'armes* scene stuck in his imagination. If he doesn't bear me a grudge, it's only because he's puzzled. He still can't understand my having treated him like a domestic animal. It's left him utterly muddled, and he stares at me as at an unreal being, a divinity. It's as though disdain, when it gets to be a certain size, really turns into a divine attribute.

"Yesterday I nearly told the duke what happened to me in the swimming pool, but I stopped myself in time, realizing that neither the duke nor any other man would ever understand it."

Rómulo was sitting on the threshold of his lodgings. The moon had risen behind the tower, and a dense elongated shadow fell across that side of the park and covered the house, the trees near it, the Republican

flag. By contrast, the rest of the park looked like a tin
bas-relief. Taking certain precautions, he walked
across to the old heating furnaces. He stayed there
over an hour, trying to find out from which angles the
furnace chimney could be seen, although during the
day—since the coals were red-hot then—not a trace
of smoke came out of it. Between this place and the
chauffeur's house there was a small poplar grove, as
well as the largest and thickest of the trimmed box
clumps. Even so, he had thought of an explanation in
case the lighted furnaces were discovered. He would
say he had set them going to clean out the water pipes,
and usually did so once a month. Perhaps one of the
militiamen would want to know where those hot-water
pipes led. In that case, Rómulo thought of saying they
supplied the ground floor of the tower—there were
several faucets there—but since this floor had at present no visible entrance, and Cartridge might possibly
want to see for himself, Rómulo went over there, removed the armorial hanging that covered the entrance,
and left the door bare and visible. It would be dangerous to have them discover a deliberately concealed
place and might stir up fresh curiosity.

These were the rooms, so he had been told, where
the mother duchess had died. Finding them kept exactly as though somebody still lived there, Rómulo
entered slowly, with misgiving. He turned on the
light. The bed was not made up, and the sheets lay
folded at the foot of it. Some women's clothes were

65

spread over the two armchairs near it, and a child's cradle stood at one side. Rómulo put his hands on a console and lifted them up with the palms full of dust. There was a strange musty smell about, and Rómulo fancied the light looked "chapelish, churchy."

If he had known those rooms had been kept intact ever since the mother duchess died—in 1905—he would have been less surprised, but even without knowing it he felt something funereal and somber. Rómulo watched the play of shadows on the old bottle-green curtains and said to himself:

"It's just as though somebody still lives here."

He was about to leave but sat down in an armchair instead, for the idea of having fathomed one of the most intimate secrets of his masters' history impressed him. As he sank into the armchair, it began creaking so much more violently than could reasonably have been expected that he got up again. He decided to go but paused nevertheless to peer into a mirror. The reflection seemed even stranger than the room. Rómulo would have said the place in the mirror was different from the one outside. The dim bedroom lights appeared far more vivid in the reflection, and the pattern of the tapestry in the background, combined with the soft glints of a cut-glass lamp, seemed to outline the shape of a person hanging in the air. Rómulo went out backward, keeping the whole scene well in view, and when he got outside he sank down on a divan, fatigued. His Andalusian peasant's sensitiveness woke in his memory glimmering legends from village days. Feeling the place was sacred, he covered the entrance again, hanging the armorial drapery and a large panoply over the door.

The hall was in twilight, and leaving the entry to those rooms concealed—just as he had found it—Rómulo went out to the main courtyard of the house and then into the park. He walked over to the lodge, but instead of going to bed he sat down near the telephone and stayed there awhile, waiting. His wife was awake. Rómulo asked her whether she knew why the lower rooms of the tower were shut up—in order to spare himself her lamentations, he did not tell her he had opened them—and she began explaining that after the mother duchess died, she had appeared to the old duke and to some of the servants as well. Balbina, who was enthralled by this subject, called to mind all the gossip gleaned from maids and flunkies during the last sixteen years and recounted how one night they had heard a noise like furniture being dragged about, and another time had noticed voices, and how, after listening closely, somebody distinctly heard the words: "I'm thirsty." Apparently the maid who used to clean these rooms went out to the park and looked in through one of the windows from the outside and saw a blue flame, tall and thin, about the height of a human being, in the middle of the bedroom. It was a very queer flame. The blue was paler

67

in some parts than in others, and it seemed to be quivering.

Rómulo listened without taking much notice. The fact that it was Balbina telling him this made it appear less likely to him. However, Rómulo remembered reading a story in a book years ago (he must still have the book at home) which had come back to his mind when he entered the mother duchess' rooms. Although the book said it was only a story, the prestige of letterpress gave it all the force of fact, for, contrary to most people, Rómulo believed that anything told in print must necessarily have happened. The story was about some rooms like these, shortly after a lady's death. The deceased's husband came in one day to look for something, and when he entered he had the same sensation as Rómulo. The place felt inhabited. A moment came when he felt sure somebody was going to walk in through the adjoining door. And, just as he was expecting it, he saw his wife appear. She was wearing a long white nightgown, and her hair—chestnut-colored—hung down loose over her back and shoulders. She walked past her husband without glancing at him and went and sat down in front of the mirror. Sitting there, she picked up a comb and held it out in her hand, offering it to him. The husband took the comb. The wife said:

"My hair hurts, and nobody comes to comb it."

The husband began combing it, and between his fingers he felt every strand of her long hair cold and

68

separate from the others. The wife complained with sighs and broken sobs. The husband would place the comb just above her forehead and draw it slowly down through her hair. He did this three, five, eight times without finding the slightest tangle. At last she rose and left again by the same door, apparently relieved, yet without speaking. As soon as he was alone, the husband backed out of the room and never wanted to live in that house again, or in that city.

Rómulo went to bed. He lay watching the shadow of the "insignia elm"—nobody knew why they called it that; the nickname had been handed down from the duchess' grandparents—in the luminous square of the window. The shadow shrank progressively as the moon rose higher. Twice the militiamen came by to change the sentry at the gate.

Rómulo fell asleep and woke late. His wife was busy with the morning chores. Her Grace had not called, and after informing his wife that he was going to the furnaces, and that if the duchess called she was to come outside and sit with a piece of white stuff on her knees as though she were sewing, Rómulo went off.

In the front part of the washhouse—a yard paved with great stone flags—stood a cherry tree. It was not a very leafy tree but fairly high. At the top there were two or three dozen cherries. Rómulo had sat down on a stone bench against the wall and was gazing at it in silence. It was pleasant to watch the birds flying to and fro and occasionally pecking at the riper cherries. The sparrows had always been his friends, and he thought he knew many of those that lived in the park. Rómulo watched them chasing one another, hopping from branch to branch. They seemed merrier under the little red globes of the cherries. When Rómulo got up to enter the adjoining enclosure where the furnaces were, a cherry fell at his feet. He retrieved it and glanced up at the birds, convinced they had picked it and thrown it down to him.

He made sure there was enough fire in the furnaces to last until ten o'clock that night. Then he went back into the little courtyard of the washhouse and before leaving sat down again for a moment. In that walled enclosure, with the cobalt sky, the ill-fitting flags between which yellowish grass was growing, he felt very far away from everything. But the tranquillity of the little courtyard was suddenly darkened by his worry lest the duchess had called while he was away from the lodge. He went outside and walked over to one of the box hedges, from the end of which he could see his own doorway. Balbina had not come out. Rómulo returned to the washhouse and sat down again on the stone bench. After a while he began to slouch sideways and eventually lay down on his back with his arms folded under his head. Seeing the sky above him and feeling all around him the quietude of "a place unknown to the militiamen," he was reminded of other such moments in his childhood and felt he was back once more in the center of himself. Again a reflection pierced that quietude:

"Had the duchess' friend come again last night?"

He dared not say her lover, but his experience as a mature man told him that at the duchess' age the nocturnal visits of a man who was neither her brother nor her father were love-visits. Rómulo kept turning over this idea—trying to imagine the clandestine visitor physically without succeeding—while he stared at the sky. He enjoyed lingering here in order to make it more probable that the duchess would have called by the time he left. Looking up into the blue sky —which was turning violet as he stared at it— Rómulo seemed to sense something liquid there, like a pond, with allusions to feminine nudity in it, just as it had happened to him in front of the seascape hanging on the wall.

The woman's nakedness appeared to Rómulo in memory as something of great purity. And he tried to understand the duchess' words in the swimming pool. It was necessary to examine carefully whether the duchess had really said what he believed he had heard. Rómulo remembered that while the duchess was speaking there had been a noise of churning water in the room and vague echoes in the lofty corners. Rómulo might have heard wrong. The duchess might have said some other words. And besides, without any need of confusion, the duchess could have said: "Rómulo a name?" and laughed. Because that name

—Rómulo—was not very often used by Spaniards, and the duchess might have laughed at the name without the slightest disrespect for the person bearing it. "Rómulo a name?" This discovery seemed to Rómulo to solve in an instant the anguish of three days. More cheerful, almost happy, he whistled softly to the birds. One of them answered. Rómulo remembered how, in the big houses of Cordova province where his father used to serve, there had always been places like this where he could escape the older folks' notice and hide away with some secret, just as he was doing now. Rómulo was still full of joy at his discovery—"Rómulo a name?"—and feeling the air beginning to cool as afternoon fell, and being unable to wait any longer, he rose and went out. The duchess had not called him, nor did she call him that day. Rómulo went to bed very late, tired out from waiting, and took a long time getting to sleep. He kept seeing the duchess' hands fluttering almost imperceptibly in the water at the ends of her open arms to keep herself afloat. He was also thinking about the washhouse, the furnace, the seascape on the wall, and all these remembrances melted into each other and formed a single torture. He muttered: "She's up there, and her lover with her. The lover makes it dangerous for her. The danger affects me, too, of course, but that doesn't matter." As he could not sleep, he ended by getting up and going into the park. Feeling almost offended because the duchess had not called him, he was at a loss what to do. His discovery regarding the duchess' sentence—"Rómulo a name?"—filled him nevertheless with glee, and he went to the basement, to the *salle d'armes,* to the swimming pool. The same water in which the duchess had bathed last time was still in it.

Rómulo walked through the shadows to the place where he had stood on the day of the incident and said aloud:

"Rómulo a man?"

Then in the same tone he added:

"Rómulo a name?"

And he proved to his own satisfaction that the two sentences sounded exactly alike. Rómulo repeated them, standing in other corners of the room. Sometimes there was an echo, and when this happened the confusion seemed greater to him. He was quite sure now that what the duchess had said was "a name" and not "a man." And this reminded him how the servants would sometimes say to him—even the butler had said it once, puzzled—"Who gave you that name?"

It did not occur to him to think that the interpretation did not morally justify her showing herself to him naked. But the latter appeared to Rómulo a miracle requiring no explanation. It had happened to him because he had a right to have it to happen to him.

He took a foil from the rack and did what he had seen López do the day the militiamen arrived; he made a stab at the lay figure. The foil had no button on the end of it, and it stuck into the dummy's cotton

73

plastron. He pulled it out and stuck it in again. It was such an energetic thrust that the point of the foil came out through the figure's back. He left it there and went slowly away. He had grown used to the dark by this time, and he gazed at the water of the swimming pool, unruffled as a mirror. "One night," he said to himself, "I'll come and bathe here."

He glimpsed a milky brightness through the high windows. Outside in the park the moon was shining. Rómulo did not condemn the duchess for receiving a man at night. He condemned the intruder, the lover. She could not be guilty. But she did not call him, she did not need him! He returned to his house depressed and went to bed.

The following days were even more difficult. Seeing that the duchess still did not call him, Rómulo fell into a state of churlish melancholy. He grew more irritable with his wife. The long sleepless nights among the shadows of the city which had been visited three or four times by the enemy air force made his insomnia more sterile. It was utterly dark on the streets, in the park. The upper floors of the neighboring houses —on the same side of the park as the front gate— sometimes had lights in their windows, but as soon as the sirens sounded they too were put out. And during the day Rómulo had to act calmly and amiably toward the four militiamen, who spent their time talking about military leaders Rómulo did not know, war incidents that meant nothing to him, political theories he did not understand. "Today I'll go up and see Her Grace," he told himself every morning, but he did not dare. The trips to the furnace continued without trouble. Sometimes he lingered in the washhouse, but the solitude there—and his secret, which was useless to him—gradually filled him with anguish. The cherry tree had lost all its fruit by now, and a few bare stones dangled from the twigs, picked clean by the birds' voracious beaks. Balbina was also worried about the duchess but in a different way. She thought she might be ill, and without even enough strength left to use the telephone.

But Rómulo kept remembering her words: "If I need you, I'll call." That meant he was not to go unless summoned.

When he had gone for two weeks—fourteen silent days—without seeing her, he decided to visit her and did so a little after midday. While he was climbing the tower stairs—from the third floor entrance—he began to feel at fault without knowing why. Yet the possibility of the duchess' reproaching him for his disobedience gave him a hidden satisfaction. When he reached the top landing he knocked at the door, but there was no answer. He pushed it open and went in. There was nobody in the anteroom. Slightly alarmed he called out:

"My Lady. . . ."

The duchess came out with the dazed eyes of someone who has just waked up. Rómulo thought: "She sleeps in the daytime." And he added: "If she sleeps in the daytime it's because she doesn't sleep at night." Rómulo thought she looked appeased, placid, in a way that revealed a happy satiety of herself and everything around her.

"You were right to come," she said, "because I was thinking of calling you today."

She went over to a table and glanced at a paper on which she had jotted something down. She ended by picking it up and giving it to Rómulo.

"You'll have to fetch all this."

Standing with the paper in his hand, Rómulo saw that the ash tray was again full of cigarette ends and that there was a burnt-out pipe lying on top of them. He felt he had been personally affronted. The duchess also wanted books, and Rómulo said he would go to the library and bring her a few dozen, but the duchess only wanted one and wrote out on a piece of paper the necessary directions for finding it. All at once Rómulo said to her somberly:

"Her Grace ought to be more careful."

"What do you mean?" she asked, surprised.

Rómulo made a great effort not to redden, and this effort made him turn pale:

"I mean I'd willingly give my life for Her Grace, if need be, but on the condition that I could save Her Grace."

She looked him up and down with even more surprise. Suddenly she said:

"Go and do as you've been told."

Rómulo went out feeling satisfied with himself. He thought of going directly to the library, but, deciding this was the most difficult task, he left it till the last.

In the cellar, he found Midge. He had taken off most of his clothes and was wearing only a ragged pair of trousers. From among the provisions that Rómulo fetched from the storeroom, he gave Midge some slices of ham and a box of crackers. Midge said to him:

"You'll have noticed that the locks are intact. I'm telling you this because I want you to know that if anything's missing from the storeroom it's not my fault."

Rómulo was puzzled:

"I didn't say anything was missing."

"If anything is missing, I'd have you know there are other living creatures in these cellars."

"Who?"

"There are rats."

Rómulo said:

"Oh. Rats."

He added that he could bring him down a cat, but Midge drew himself up on his short legs:

"Fortunately, there aren't many rats, but there's not a cat in Madrid capable of facing a single one of them."

"Are they as big as all that?"

Midge puffed out his chest again—a chest that

seemed to begin somewhere about his knees—and said:

"Two of them are nearly as big as me."

Rómulo looked at him without understanding how he could talk of the matter with pride. Midge added, hitching his trousers:

"They come after Their Graces' food."

As Rómulo walked away, he could hear him still muttering. He cocked his ears and caught a few disjointed words:

"Luckily, I'm here . . . they'll have to deal with me."

When the food and bottles had been brought up to the duchess' rooms, Rómulo noticed the ash tray was clean. "After what I told her, she realized this detail was giving her away." The duchess reminded him that he had not fetched the book, and Rómulo went to the library. When he arrived, he saw that the light coming through the long lattice-covered windows was "churchy," like the light in the mother duchess' bedroom. The high vaulted ceiling had frescoes painted on it. A figure symbolizing Fame, with a long trumpet, was floating among several naked women in a blue sky, and they all seemed to detach themselves from the ceiling and fly about. The harmonious medley of rosy flesh and blue background renewed the scene in the swimming pool. Rómulo came out of his abstraction and looked at the duchess' note on the piece of

78

paper. Thousands and thousands of books were lined up in all directions, in front of him, behind him, and on both sides, and Rómulo felt lost, thinking he would never be able to find the one he was looking for. He turned round and round, and the more he looked in all directions the less he saw. He started off to read the note again. Ah, first he had to hunt for the author's name and the title in the files kept in a cabinet on the left coming in. It was some time before he found the files, and when at last he discovered them it was getting dark, and he turned on the electric light. Afterward he looked for the shelf, found it, and took out a book numbered seventy-two. He opened the cover and saw that the title and the author were the same as those in the duchess' note. But the book was shabby, its covers dulled, its edges worm-eaten. The inner pages were made of coarse paper and seemed dirty to him. Rómulo was not satisfied, and, thinking to take her another, better-looking, book, he glanced about near by and took down the one that appeared most sumptuous to him. It was small, bound in white leather, with silver letters on the outside, and the author, according to what it said there, was a marquis. All this seemed quite adequate, and he was preparing to leave when he noticed a photograph in a cut-glass frame on one of the tables. It was a recent photo of the duchess. Rómulo stopped to gaze at it, and it was only when he heard a clock on the wall striking the hour—ten— that he realized he must return to the tower. As the framed portrait would not go into his pocket, he kept it in his hands with the books. He was leaving and just about to turn off the lights when he heard footsteps outside, and before he had time to think who it might be the duchess appeared.

"Can't you find the book?"

She went over to Rómulo and took the whole packet out of his hands, including the portrait. Seeing it, the duchess glanced at Rómulo—it was a look as quick as lightning and as disturbingly luminous—and put the portrait back on the table. The duchess said nothing about that, but with the two books in her hand—the marquis' on top—asked:

"Why did you take this other one?"

"I don't know. I thought it seemed nicer and cleaner."

It was one of the Marquis de Sade's books. The duchess repressed a smile in the left corner of her mouth.

"Haven't you opened it?"

"No, My Lady."

That edition had licentious pictures in it. The duchess' husband valued it highly. The duchess looked at her own portrait again, picked it up to take with her, and said:

"Go into the corridor ahead of me. If you suspect there's anyone around, cough twice. If the way's clear, once."

Rómulo pulled out his weapon, cocked it, and held

it inside his coat pocket. The mechanical way he did it gave the duchess a feeling of real danger.

Before reaching the tower stairs the duchess dismissed him, saying once more:

"I think it would be better if you didn't come to my rooms unless I call you."

Rómulo was thinking: "She's afraid I'll surprise her with the other man." He went out into the park. On catching sight of him, the sentry—it was López—remarked: "What's the duke got to say for himself?" Rómulo replied with a grunt. He did not care for the joke.

A few more days went by without the duchess' calling him. One morning, remembering what the duchess had said about the Marquis de Sade's book—"Have you opened it? Did you look inside?"—Rómulo recalled having seen beside that book, on the same shelf, three others exactly like it, with the very same marquis' name on their backs. He thought about this until he could no longer contain his curiosity and then returned to the library.

Near the place where the duchess' portrait had been he noticed a silver paperweight. It was the figure of a nude woman. The graceful curves gleamed softly in the light. He stroked the little sculpture with his hand, and the touch of it was too cold. He clutched it convulsively until it became tempered to the warmth of his peasant's hand. Afterward he went on toward the shelves, without letting go of the silver figurine, and took out the three books which identically resembled the duchess'. On the white leather binding he read: *Marquis de Sade, I—Marquis de Sade, III—Marquis de Sade, IV.* He sat down and opened them at random. He found a surprising illustration. A man and a woman lying together. In this and other illustrations the artist had had no compunction in showing the crudest details. Rómulo felt shocked and puzzled. Books had always been associated in his mind with a respect for morals and religious virtue. The sudden glimpse of those pictures disconcerted him. To Rómulo, amorous intimacy was first and foremost a secret thing. Seeing this book (printed and published and therefore available to everybody), he did not know what to think. In one of the other volumes the figures sometimes appeared dressed. A man was trussing up his mistress' skirts while she waited in an attitude of indolent expectation. Rómulo felt in the thick of scandal. But once in it, he had to come out of it with an opinion. What was he to think of all this? Rómulo wanted to read these books, but he was stopped when the idea cropped up in his mind that he would never be able to enter the duke's and duchess' secret world. He left the books where he had found them and went out thinking: "There's not a woman in the world who'd dare receive a book like that from the hands of anyone who wasn't her lover or her husband. And much less dare to laugh just as she was receiving it." The duchess had smiled. Hadn't it been an immensely

82

confident smile? Or perhaps the duchess had again behaved toward him as though neither modesty nor reserve were necessary? And starting to interpret it all once more, Rómulo said to himself: "It's only natural. What can I expect after that morning in the *salle d'armes*?" For by now he no longer believed she had said "a name" instead of "a man."

He went out into the park with the Marquis de Sade's illustrations on his mind. The duchess' nakedness in the swimming pool was taking on a different meaning. He seemed to be holding her in his clenched hand, like the silver figurine, but instead of being cold she was fiery and burned him. Halfway through the afternoon he went to feed the furnace and afterward crossed the park and walked over toward the militiamen. Ever since early morning a slight rumbling noise had been coming from the horizon, which he thought was a storm at first (the sky was overcast), but the militiamen told him it was the artillery. The militiamen were less expansive than usual, all except Cartridge, who seemed gay and excited at the enemy's nearness. Once again Rómulo had to remind himself, in already familiar fashion, that it would be unwise to visit the tower. But next day in the morning he gave up thinking about it and went there. Cannon fire could still be heard in the distance.

"Everything seems to be lost, My Lady," he said without apologizing for his visit.

"I'd say the contrary, Rómulo."

"That depends," he said in a tone of hostile reserve that surprised him, "from which side you're looking at it."

The duchess stood staring at him a moment as though she did not know what to reply. She saw he was resentful and could not imagine it was because she had not called him. At last she said:

"It's surprising to hear you talk like that."

Rómulo avoided looking at the seascape hanging on the wall. The sky glimpsed through the windows was leaden gray. The open door onto the terrace framed its ashen paving and a corner of the balustrade, which was gray, too. Everything seemed flattened out by the natural sunless light of that day. Rómulo noticed there were no cigarette ends in the ash tray, but next to it on the table he saw a little fresh ash. A tiny little cylinder of gray ash, almost white. Having observed that the duchess' footsteps left a mark on the carpet, he began looking round for masculine traces as well, but she sat down and invited him to be seated opposite her. It was the first time she had been so considerate to him, and Rómulo would not accept. The duchess remained in doubt as to whether his refusal meant enmity or respect. Neither spoke, and finally the duchess said:

"If you think the same as my enemies, Rómulo, you ought to remember that I said you were quite free to go the first day."

Rómulo appeared to hesitate before answering. At last he said:

"It was different then."

The duchess adopted a protective attitude:

"Rómulo, you've never seriously thought of taking sides, either then or now."

Rómulo went on looking cautiously at the carpet. This attitude seemed very timid to the duchess. But Rómulo was looking for male footprints. He believed he had found one near the bedroom door, where the slanting light from the window showed up the carpet pattern more clearly. The duchess continued:

"I understand your position, because in some ways it's rather like my own. But I'll tell you the truth. You've waited till now to take sides, and now you've decided in favor of the losers. That means you're desperate, and I'm sorry."

Still Rómulo did not speak, and the duchess added:

"The rest doesn't matter. You can be red or green or blue if you like. All I ask you is not to declare it openly, because our people are going to be hard some day about exacting responsibilities. Don't forget that those men who want you to be a Red today may be the first to accuse you tomorrow. Don't trust anybody, Rómulo."

The duchess changed her tone and assumed a familiar manner:

"Did the Requisition Junta pay your wages last month?"

85

"No, My Lady."

The duchess groped among some papers at a small desk, signed a check, and gave it to him with the warning that she had put a date previous to the civil war on it. "You must say you've had this check for over two months."

That little scrap of paper in his hand upset and offended Rómulo. He was looking at the masculine footprint on the carpet near the bedroom and remembering the licentious illustrations. A wave of anger rose to his lips.

"My Lady," he said, "I get my wages from the Junta, not from you, and whether the Junta pays me or not is my own business and none of yours."

The duchess smiled, without taking his words seriously, and said in a voice in which there was a certain impish humor:

"Rómulo, I didn't mean to offend you."

His silence was deeply bitter. That little scrap of paper in his hand was a mockery, too. He did not know why, but the idea of being paid—when what was being aired between them was her life, his own—filled him with shame. Rómulo tore up the check; he ripped it into small pieces and threw them on the floor. He started to go without offering any apology. The duchess called him back and asked him in the friendliest manner to pick up those little bits of paper and not oblige her to do it. Rómulo obeyed. Not as a servant, he was telling himself, but for **chivalry's sake. He** realized that this attitude—bending down, picking up paper—was the humblest a human being can adopt. In the air Rómulo felt the presence of some force before which he did not want to give way, did not want to retreat. Against this enemy force, the only resource that remained to him was to be "a Red." There was in the tower an atmosphere forbidden to him, as forbidden as before the war, with the addition that it stayed secret and enclosed within its secrecy something like a threat. A very tenuous voice was coming from the radio, a voice that admitted the Republican troops were losing ground and warned that the fall and loss of Madrid, although highly deplorable, would be only an incident in the struggle and by no means the end of the war.

Rómulo went out very annoyed with himself. He could not understand—once away from the duchess' presence—what he had done, what he had said.

From the duchess' diary:

"Rómulo's afraid. His fear takes the form of defiance, and it's so strong that it pushes him in just the opposite direction from the one prudence would advise.

"The duke comes every night and believes victory is a matter of hours.

"I've just been reading some of the letters he wrote in the King's time, and in the middle of all that's happening now they seem almost ridiculous with their superficial problems and empty chatter."

87

The duchess was feeling nervous for the first time. Every now and then the din of the battle sounded so close she would have thought her friends were already inside the city.

Rómulo, also excited by the nearness of the fighting, wandered about in the park like a ghost, his mind filled with the lewd pictures in the Marquis de Sade's books and with a growing and aimless rancor. The next night he decided to watch the secret entrances to the palace, which the militiamen did not know. But he saw nothing. Two nights later, after posting himself in various spots in the neighborhood, he saw an individual getting down from an ambulance a few blocks away and going toward an old servants' entrance, which communicated with the tower. The furtive lover arrived every evening about the same time and left a little before dawn.

Rómulo was gloomy and sullen. He did not speak to the militiamen except to make evasive and sometimes impertinent remarks. One night he waited hidden in a corner of the staircase by which the unknown man went up. He was there for several hours. About midnight he heard his wife calling him at the park gates, but he did not move. "What's the woman doing out there so late? Why's she yelling like that? Why doesn't she go to bed?" A little later he saw the door open and a shadow enter cautiously. Rómulo shoved the pistol against his back and told him to put up his hands. At the same time he had a feeling there was something familiar about the individual's outline.

"Come on, Rómulo," said the duke, breathing with some difficulty. "It's only I. Just see what a fright you've given me!"

Rómulo was so disconcerted that the duke felt obliged to say:

"I'm not a ghost. But to have them believing I'm dead is the best thing that could happen to me, and you mustn't tell anyone you've seen me."

Rómulo, putting the pistol back, stammered:

"Who'd have thought it, My Lord? I was here to protect Her Grace."

He began explaining what had happened in the house during the last month and a half, but the duke was not listening to him:

"I know all about it."

"But Her Grace's position. . . ."

The duke disappeared up the stairs without hearing him, and Rómulo returned to the park very depressed. He walked over to his house. He went to bed without undressing. Afterward he got up again and went out once more. The duke was alive. And by now the city was being attacked along the whole east side, from the Ciudad Universitaria to the Cerro de los Angeles. These facts seemed to him to be secretly related. At night the thundering of the artillery sounded much nearer.

He went toward the tower. "Sooner or later the duke's sure to be discovered. Perhaps the police are following him already? If that's so, why does he come here? Why does he get Her Grace involved? Does he want to make her share his own loss and ruin?" He walked about near the palace walls, the front door, his shoulders hunched and his movements heavy. Then he went farther off and looked up at the top windows of the tower.

He wandered about in this way all night, remembering the duchess and thinking he could see her naked between the shadows cast by the trees on the lower windowpanes. "The duchess is sure to have spoken to her husband about me and told him what's been happening these last few days. Above all, she must have told him I tore up the check. I didn't tell her clearly why I did it, but His Grace may think I did it as an act of enmity and rebelliousness because I don't want to be in the pay of my enemies." Rómulo enjoyed the idea of the duke's thinking this and other things about him. And he listened to the bursts of cannon fire, which sometimes made one of the panes in the downstairs windows of his lodgings rattle in an incomprehensible fashion, for occasionally the vibration came from the more distant reports and not from the nearer ones.

He went to the militiamen's sleeping quarters. All three of them woke up with a start. In that start, Rómulo thought he discerned yet another proof of how dangerous the situation was. Rómulo sat down on Ruiz' bed and said he wanted to know with what crimes the Duke of Alcanadre was charged. Ruiz protested indignantly against being waked up to be asked about such a thing, but observing something abnormal in Rómulo he changed his attitude at once. He began enumerating military and political crimes.

"What would happen," asked Rómulo, "if it turned out he was still alive and they caught him?"

Ruiz sat up:

"Eight hours later he'd be stood up against a wall."

López said, lowering his voice confidentially:

"Where is he?"

Rómulo restrained them:

"Don't ask me anything, because just now I don't know myself, but if I have any luck I'll be able to hand him over before morning."

Rómulo went out to the street and walked about in the neighborhood. Since he was afraid that someone might see him, it was some time before he decided to approach the tower stairs. When he finally became convinced there was nobody either at the windows or on the street, he went and stood at the foot of the stairs in the same place as last time. While he was waiting, the sirens sounded an air-raid alarm. Beyond the high dusty-paned window, the searchlights furrowed the sky, making it look like a coarse fabric with a shifting weave. At the same time the machine guns and anti-aircraft batteries had opened fire, and the tracers could be seen shooting up like rosaries of Bengal lights. One cannon sounded so near that Rómulo would

91

have said it was in the park. But he kept his mind on the staircase.

"Now," he said, "in the confusion of the bombardment, the duke'll see his opportunity and come out."

When the latter appeared and saw Rómulo, he said: "Hello, Rómulo. You still here?"

Rómulo asked in an equally composed voice:

"Don't you think these visits are dangerous for Her Grace?"

The duke went over to the window and looked at the sky without answering. He asked Rómulo to go onto the street and see if there was anyone about. Rómulo went, and, as soon as he was alone again, with the duke's voice—a satisfied lover's voice—in his ears, he said to himself: "I'm a coward. The duke's risking his life. And what about me? What am I risking? I'm a coward. And cowardice'll be the end of me, since the militiamen are already on their guard because of what I told them. And if I'm killed, what'll happen to Her Grace without me?" But, even so, he added: "At this very moment, hundreds of people are dying who are no better or worse than the duke." He returned.

"Is the master armed?"

The duke thought there was some difficulty on the street and drew his revolver. Rómulo struck him a blow on the hand, and the revolver flew through the air and fell somewhere in the darkness. In a changed voice quivering with savage wrath, he roared:

"Go out ahead of me!"

The duke flung himself on Rómulo, who tripped over the first step of the staircase as he retreated and fell down. The duke had the upper hand and managed to grip him between his strong rider's knees.

"A traitor in my house, eh?" he said. "I was hoping our police would hang you, but now I'll have the pleasure of doing it myself."

Feeling the duke's hands at his throat, Rómulo saw he was lost. "I must kill him," he thought with a strange calmness. And, without knowing where he was aiming, he fired. The bullet went through one of the duke's knees. Rómulo took advantage of the wounded man's surprise to wrench himself free. The duke tried without succeeding to get up and growled:

"Now what have you done, you idiot?"

Rómulo went over and helped him up. When the duke was on his feet again, Rómulo shoved the pistol against his back and pushed him with it. He said in a voice from which the violence had already disappeared: "His Grace must keep quiet and do as I say." The duke went forward limpingly. Rómulo muttered at him:

"Get outside. I'm going to hand you over to them. When they make you testify at the trial, sir, you're not to say anything to anybody about Her Grace and the tower."

The duke was dragging one leg. Once on the street,

Rómulo led him toward the park gates, to reach which
they had to walk about a hundred yards and turn a
corner. The duke stopped and faced Rómulo. The
latter retreated a step and raised his armed hand to
the height of the duke's chest. With an immense effort
the duke tried to take a conciliatory attitude:

"Rómulo. . . ."

But he could get no further; his intention was
swamped in rage. He seized Rómulo by the forearm
with both hands, deflecting the weapon and trying to
grab it away from him. He would have succeeded, but
Rómulo fired twice, and the shots brought the sentry
running out, with the three other militiamen behind
him. When the duke saw them he tried to flee, but his
wound made it difficult, and they surrounded him.
Cartridge looked the duke in the face and said to him:

"I suppose you know what'll happen to you?"

"Yes. The same as to you," replied the duke. "Today I'll be killed, and tomorrow you'll be killed."

The militiamen took the duke away to Police Headquarters. Only Estradera remained in the park. When
Rómulo saw them all disappear up the Calle de
Segovia, he returned to the tower stairs and searched
about on the floor until he found the duke's weapon.
Afterward he went to his lodgings. It was still dark.
Everything had happened in a few minutes. He found
his wife sleeping peacefully. He went out again and
walked over to the tower. "I've done my duty," he
thought calmly. The air-raid alarm was over. Rómulo

mounted the stairs with a firm tread. He paused and
sat down on a step. Before seeing the duchess he
wanted to make a summary of his own position: "As
soon as she sees me, the duchess'll guess the whole
thing, because she must have heard the shot on the
staircase.

"She heard the ones on the street, too, and she must
have connected them with the duke.

"Personally, I feel as if twenty years had been
lifted from me.

"The militiamen say the war will last a long time.

"It might last four or five years.

"The way things are now, four years is a lifetime.

"The duchess heard the shots, and she's waiting for
me. She's waiting for me because she needs me."

He felt absolutely happy. He went on up. At the top
there was a landing giving onto the hall doorway.
Rómulo knocked and entered without waiting for an
answer. He found the duchess pressed against one of
the windows, trying to guess what was happening
from the noises outside. When she caught sight of
Rómulo she questioned him with her eyes, making no
attempt to hide her fear of his answer. Rómulo took
his time about replying.

"I hope," she said with frightened uncertainty, "the
duke's safe."

Before answering, Rómulo sat down in an armchair
uninvited, and when he was seated he said, looking at
the blue seascape hanging on the wall:

"It isn't easy for a man with a bullet through his knee to go very far."

The duchess stared about her, stunned.

"Did the men on guard catch him?"

"Yes, My Lady."

"Did they take him away?"

Rómulo nodded. The duchess was in such a state of tension that she seemed to be projecting her whole life outward, through her eyes.

"Where have they taken him?"

Rómulo said slowly, with perfect serenity:

"They've taken him to Police Headquarters. They didn't want to take him to the district committee, because he seemed an important catch to them. It's only natural. Her Grace understands."

She spoke like a sleepwalker:

"To the district committee. . . ."

Rómulo rectified:

"No, My Lady. To Police Headquarters. They say the trial generally lasts eight hours."

The duchess gazed at him without speaking. Rómulo said nothing either. She had one bare foot on the carpet. It was as small and chubby as a child's. Beginning with that foot, Rómulo reconstructed the whole of the duchess' nudity and had to look away from her. With a trembling voice the duchess was saying:

"Don't just sit there, Rómulo. Go and help him. I'll give you a fortune. I'll give you anything you want.

Fix it up with those militiamen and do something to help him."

The duchess repeated these words with a vague wandering stare and without the least faith in Rómulo's listening to her. Without the least faith in what she was saying, either. Rómulo realized this and answered in an indolent tone:

"Her Grace will understand that, as things are now, neither I nor anybody else can do anything."

She was looking at him, thinking: "How can he help the duke, he in particular? Why am I asking him to help the duke?" She could not keep silent. The tension which had previously been apparent in her eyes —a faithless tension—had begun to die down; her gaze was no longer luminous, and all her discouragement came out in her voice, which tried to sound energetic and accusing but was only wan.

"Haven't you any weapons?" she asked. "But weapons or no weapons, I know you've got a right to be cowardly."

Rómulo smiled. The duchess considered him cowardly, but he had a right to smile in the depths of his hard secret victory, and he said:

"They'd kill me. Life doesn't much matter to me, as Her Grace knows, but I think—though perhaps I'm going too far in thinking. . . ."

Rómulo paused, glancing at the carpet, the ceiling.

"Perhaps I've no right to think that. . . ."

He looked her in the face, nerving himself.

97

"Please understand, My Lady. As things are, what would Her Grace do without me?"

She looked at him with startled attention, as if she were suddenly afraid of him.

"Without you? But I can't bear your presence! Don't you realize I can't bear it?"

Rómulo looked at her ironically.

"Very well. I'll go, if Her Grace wishes."

But he did not go. The duchess walked over to the half-opened window. In the distance the sky was beginning to lighten. She stood there in silence, occasionally making mechanical gestures—brushing a lock of hair back from her temples, picking up something or other and putting it down again—gestures with which she tried to relieve her inner anguish. Raising her voice in a terrible way, she said:

"You're not the one who's to blame for all this."

Rómulo was puzzled.

"Keep calm, My Lady. Remember they might hear you."

"All the better. Let them hear me. What else can I do, except shout the truth to the four winds?"

She was by the window and seemed ready to go on shouting when Rómulo came to her and covered her mouth with his hand. She swung round with a protesting movement, and Rómulo took her by the shoulders and pressed her head and her whole body gently against him. He refused to let her scream, yet Rómulo would have liked to hear that "truth" she wanted to tell the world about her enemies through the window. The duchess drew away from him. Rómulo was livid. She did not seem offended. It had all happened naturally. Rómulo's touch had restored her calm. The duchess began speaking again in a low voice, apparently composed:

"For heaven's sake, Rómulo, go away."

Rómulo did not go away. He felt grateful to her for her nerves, her frenzy, the way she had let herself go.

"Go away and don't come back any more!"

Rómulo went slowly toward the elevator. He fetched it up. He opened it carefully, went inside, and before closing it said to the duchess:

"Does Her Grace want me to bring her anything?"

The duchess thought there was some irony in those words, glanced at him in fear, and made no answer. As soon as she was alone, she began pacing from the terrace door to the lift door, without knowing what she was doing, until well after sunrise. She saw the duke's letters on the desk—the faraway letters of their courtship days—tied up with blue ribbons. She dared not touch them. To go and take refuge in the duke's letters now would be like seeking "a widow's" comfort. For some moments she felt deep horror. "I'm beginning to see life as it really is," she said to herself. "I never would have imagined it was like this. I'm frightened." She started pacing again, thinking: "It's all too frightful for me to be able to take it as a lesson, and even if it wasn't, that kind of lesson is no use to me by now, perhaps because I came into life to play and I'm fated to go on playing till the end. But there's blood in my game. There's blood now." She sank down on the bed and fell fast asleep.

It was ten o'clock in the morning when a shell burst on the terrace and tore up part of the paving. It also smashed the lower part of the door leading from the balcony to the bedroom. The duchess woke up and rushed out to the hall in terror. A little later on, more composed, she went over to the terrace and peered about to see how much damage had been done. She noticed that some bits of shrapnel had entered the bedroom and one of them was sticking in the ceiling. She returned to the hall. She gathered up some papers and a few clothes and went down to the floor below. She made sure the windows in these rooms were shut, turned on the lights, and, glancing about frightened, said to herself: "It's just as if that shell dropped and burst on the terrace because Rómulo willed it. He seems to have chased me out of those rooms up there, and now I've come down to these other ones, running away and waiting. Running away from him. And waiting for him."

CHAPTER
THREE

RÓMULO WENT OUT TO THE STREET TO SEE IF
the militiamen were coming back. He stayed
a while talking to the sentry, and after they
had exchanged a few vague words and ordinary sentences and he realized they would inevitably have to
mention the duke's being denounced and captured, he
returned slowly to the park. He felt hungry and went
over to his lodgings. But he paused on the threshold,
hesitant. Then, unhurriedly, he walked across the park
toward the palace. Without knowing why, he headed
for the basement.

As he neared the *salle d'armes*, he seemed to be
nearing the duke himself. He had him on his mind.
He was seeing him on the staircase a few hours ago.
"I spoke to him, and he didn't answer me." Then he
saw himself in front of the duchess and heard her say:

101

"You're not to blame; no." What did she mean by that? Did she know what had happened? Did she realize the way everything had taken place?

Although the darkness was less dense here, the *salle d'armes* was also in vague uniform twilight. The pool was full of water, and it was the same water as on "that day." Rómulo began undressing. When he was bare from the waist up, he saw his broad chest opposite him in the same mirror where the duchess used to see herself. He saw his image without being able to see the mirror, as though another Rómulo peered back at him from the depths of a blind window. Rómulo checked himself when he was about to unfasten his trousers. The idea of swimming here seemed unworthy now. He noticed a stilly gleam in the water, and felt frightened, as if the little pool were so deep no swimmer would ever be able to touch the bottom with his feet.

He moved away from the pool. He heard murmurs in the park and listened attentively. Since he had handed over the duke, any noise startled him and put him on his guard. He had a feeling that unexpected and perhaps fearful things might happen because of what he had done. Cannon sounded in the distance. He enjoyed the fatal compulsion of the blood and fire they were all under. He turned on a lamp at the foot of one of the racks. There was the dummy with the foil stuck in its chest. The dummy had the duke's slim

upright bearing. Rómulo tried to pull the foil out of
its chest, but, when he pulled it, the dummy, which
was very tall, leaned down over him, and Rómulo let
go of the foil and retreated a step. Seeing two other
foils on the ground, he picked them up and put them
in the rack. On the shelf underneath, there was a little
parchment-bound book with iron clasps shaped like
chimeras. On the back, in big lapidary lettering, it
said: *Booke of the Examples of Monarchies.* The first
chapter was headed by a naked man and woman. A
small branch crossed over the man's belly, and her
hair hung down over one shoulder onto her thighs
with the same modest intent. It was Adam and Eve,
both of them with the silly faces of figures in wood-
cuts.

Rómulo found a sprig of fern, still quite fresh, between two of the pages and some pencil-marked sentences in the same place, with the following note in
the duchess' hand: "See further on page 103." He
closed the book and held it in his hands while he
watched the light beginning to enter through the long
windows.

"Now," he said to himself again, "the militiamen
won't suspect me, and Her Grace will be safer."

He was still naked from the waist up and stood
staring at the water in the swimming pool. He approached it, knelt, and went down on all fours meaning to wet his face and hair; but, when he lifted his
cupped hands full of water to his face, instead of

103

washing with it, he drank it. He drank three, four, five more times. Then he dressed, picked up the *Booke of the Examples of Monarchies* to take to the duchess, who was doubtless reading it, because the sprig of fern was still green, and went to the cellar to see Midge.

The dwarf was intrigued by the constant cannonading and the shots he had heard the previous night: one pistol shot in the house and two more on the street. With his eyes reddened like a ferret's, Midge said:

"There's fighting going on everywhere. In the park, on the street, out in the country, up in the air, and down in the cellar. In the cellar, too."

"Here? In the cellar?" Rómulo asked.

"Yes. Here, too."

"How?" said Rómulo, glancing around.

"There's a rat that tries to defy me."

"And you fight it?"

"Yes."

"How?"

"Tooth and nail. Kicking and biting."

Rómulo frowned. Was the rat as big as all that?

"It's a rat bigger than two gelded cats, and it goes for me. Come over here."

He took him across to the storeroom door, which was lined with zinc. The door bore traces of having been scratched, and there was a small heap of lime on the floor. The midget said:

"The one that works here is Chrissie."

With sudden condescension toward himself, the midget added:

"Well, that's what I call her."

Rómulo said:

"She must be big."

The midget led him to the other side of the door and showed him a small hole:

"See how the cement's broken here? Well, they've managed to bore right through it and reach the earth. They're trying to make a gallery to get into the store-room. They're good workers, eh?"

"Looks like it."

"Especially Chrissie. The other, the one that works here, is not so quick. Besides, he's got two broken claws. But he's very brave. It's a male, and I call him Gimlet."

Rómulo did not know what to say. He looked at Midge and noticed some swastika crosses traced here and there on the wall. The dwarf entertained himself as best he could.

"Tell Their Graces," he said. "Tell Their Graces there's somebody fighting for them down here."

Rómulo pointed to the swastikas.

"And that thing, what is it?"

"Against the Jews."

To Rómulo, the word "Jew" did not mean a race, or even a religion. He thought it was a synonym for money-lender.

"But there aren't any."

"Any what?"

"Jews."

"Aren't there? All right. Then it's there so they won't come. I'm in favor of their not coming."

Rómulo still did not understand, but he realized that a creature like Midge was privileged to say weird things. The midget repeated:

"Tell Their Graces."

Rómulo left and went out to the park. He walked over toward the beds of autumn flowers, and, finding them thick with green buds as yet unopened, he thought to himself: "Those roses will be opening between today and tomorrow, and they're all white or yellow ones. As they haven't opened yet, nobody's seen them, and nobody'll know if I cut them now, though there are more than six dozen of them." He took out his knife and started cutting them, leaving the stems very long. When he had finished, he went over to the washhouse and left them there wrapped up in a piece of damp sacking with a trickle of water dribbling over it. Everything—the stems, the water, the buds—was movingly fresh and light. Within the green calyx, the still closed petals must have the same purity as the skin on the duchess' belly. "Surely," he thought, "the duchess must have got over her first spasm, and grown used to the idea of the duke's being dead." He was smiling. He told himself that next day the flowers would be at their best, half-opened, some of them full blown, and then he would take them to the duchess. Now that her nightly visitor had disappeared, it might be possible to talk to her, a thing he had not really tried to do up till now. So that the militiamen should not see the flowers, he would take the buds over to the elevator that night and leave them there in a bucket of water. The following day he would have only to go up. He would fill the duchess' rooms with flowers. He had a right to do so—he told himself— just as he had a right to forbid the duchess to shout. He wanted to ask her not to shout the truth from the window, but to tell it to him, instead, in private. "After what's happened, after my handing over the duke, she means a grave danger to me in future, perhaps quite soon." This danger pleased him. He remembered his last visit to the duchess: "When I came in she was looking out the window." What could she see from the window, except the darkness of night? But the shots had lit up that darkness in the park. "I was walking about in that darkness out there, and she knew it. She was thinking about me while she was watching that darkness. I'll put flowers in that darkness tomorrow." He heard the water falling over the flowers with a gracious sound, like the fountains in his childhood. "She'd like his lordship to be safe. Safe? And who's safe in this world? She knows it was my hand that pushed him up against the wall, where the soldiers do target practice. She knows the same hand later pushed her body against mine, and that this hand's ready to do anything, if only some

107

day she'll kiss it between a caress on her naked bosom and another on her hair. She knows it."

Rómulo made sure that not even a wisp of smoke was coming out of the chimney. "She said she'd give me a fortune, that she'd give me anything I wanted. Anything I wanted." A lizard was climbing up over the stones in the wall. It crawled a little, stopped, began crawling again. It, too, seemed to be listening to the cannon and hesitating before going on. As for the birds, they had disappeared, they had all gone away during the first days of the battle of Madrid. "The duchess told me I had weapons. Asked me why I didn't use them. I've got more weapons than I believed myself. And I do use them. She doesn't know it, or maybe she knows it too well, and perhaps that's why she said she couldn't stand my presence. But what I know is that she not only listens to me now, she talks to me, too, she lets herself go in front of me and wants to shout out the truth, a truth I know already, because you don't shout her kind of truth, you don't say it. You see it. Every time I lay my eyes on her I see the whole of her truth."

Rómulo was aware of his solitude in that peaceful spot, with the breeze blowing coolly against his head. "The flowers will finish opening in the tower, under Her Grace's eyes."

In his own fashion, Rómulo had studied the ways of flowers, and he believed he had come to understand

108

them and have a talking relationship with them. One of his earliest surprises in observing flowers came when he noticed how they sometimes made movements. Not movements of growth or opening, which depend on outside things such as sun, water, spring, or autumn, but other movements that seemed to respond to an inner will. Rómulo had spent hours and hours watching a bank of calla lilies, sometimes seeing a bee or a hornet entering their deep funnels. Occasionally there were big velvety bumblebees among them, robed in Asiatic splendor and moving with a certain religious gravity. And he had seen one of these bumblebees go slowly into the flower's womb like a king into his chamber, and when it was inside he had observed how one of the flower's stamens had moved downward and touched the bumblebee on the back, staining him with yellow. The apparent purpose in the flower had left Rómulo perplexed.

He could imagine nothing superior in human life to the slow entry, little by little, of one of these insects into the womb of a half-opened rose, a magnolia, a snapdragon. That penetration, with its delicacy of touch, sight, smell, and taste all mingled in a single feeling, was something that man could not experience, that man could only imagine. Rómulo knew there were male and female flowers. He had often fertilized a female flower with his hand, taking pollen from male stamens. "For everything," he would say, "wants to be fulfilled, and should be," and leaving the fertilization of a flower to the wind or insects seemed to him at times too hazardous and casual.

When he walked back through the park he felt like the owner of it. For many years he had known that, every evening in autumn, the first star came out above the highest tree in the park, over toward the wash-house corner, and faded every morning—until the middle of November—behind his house (now behind the Republican flag), whereas the sun appeared every day above the wall between the two distant lines of buildings that vanished toward the Plaza del Progreso. If the militiamen never returned, and he stayed here alone with all this and with the duchess as well, he would feel like those bumblebees slowly entering a magnolia's womb.

But the militiamen came back accompanied by five more persons: two officers and three sergeants. Ruiz hurried forward to explain to him:

"They're going to set up a recruiting office here, and a training center for antitank units."

Rómulo asked, stunned:

"How many men?"

But they did not answer. Seeing all these people scurrying about, Rómulo had a sudden feeling that it was all over with the duchess. One of the officers was called Ordóñez. The other one, who always looked annoyed but was quite affable when he spoke, was called Uriarte. Rómulo warned them there was no coal and that without heat the house was very chilly in winter. "If there's no coal, at least there's plenty of wood," said Ordóñez, laughing.

Before even seeing the palace, they had decided to stay there. "They'll bring enough blankets and mattresses," said Ordóñez, "for a hundred men, and tomorrow we'll start it all going." And he added, addressing Rómulo:

"Don't pull such a long face, you there!"

It was a question of two different organizations: a recruiting office for volunteers, who would be assigned that same day to various barracks to be trained, and the antitank company that would live in the ground-floor rooms of the palace. Rómulo offered his own house for the recruiting office, wanting to keep people away from the tower as much as possible. Ordóñez considered this adequate, since the house was near the park gates.

They went over the main building together, and when they reached the third floor Lieutenant Ordóñez began mounting the tower stairs. Rómulo made a violent effort to hold his nerves in check. The lieutenant walked past the door to the fourth floor, where the duchess was, and went on up. On reaching the top floor he entered, and Rómulo, who did not know the duchess had gone down to the floor below, followed him with the pistol in his hand, telling himself: "When he sees the duchess, I'll have to kill him." But she was neither in the hall nor on the terrace. His hands shaking, Rómulo put the pistol back without letting go of it. "Is she in the bathroom?" The officer stepped out onto the terrace, saw the destruction caused by the shell, and picked up a bit of shrapnel. "It was from a five-inch gun," he said. Then he glanced down at the places overlooked by the tower and without saying a word more went in again, followed by Rómulo, who kept his hand in his coat pocket and the pistol in his hand. Again they passed the fourth-floor door. "It's funny," thought Rómulo, "that her ladyship isn't up here. If she's in the bathroom, she doesn't know she saved this officer's life by hiding." He could not understand either how a shell had burst on the terrace without his learning of it. It was all absurd and incredible. Uriarte was waiting for them downstairs to finish fixing up the recruiting office. Everything was ready that night, and next day the radio announced it was the seventeenth recruiting center for volunteers from the district.

In spite of everything, Rómulo managed to find an opportunity to go to the washhouse, fetch the flowers, and take them over to the elevator, where he left them without being seen. The arrangements for billeting the officers and for the future quarters of the men who would arrive next day left the right wing of the building fairly free. Rómulo saw they meant to use the small side entrances on the left—kitchens, servants' dining-room, pantries—keeping the front door locked, because—as Ordóñez said—if they took to using that door the house would be an icebox in winter.

Rómulo wanted to go to the tower and bring the duchess the news that the duke was no longer alive. He went up, waited, called from the stairs. He came running down to the floor below and found her in the hall with a fur coat over her pajamas. The rooms were the same as those above, except for the furnishings and the fact that the terrace space was taken up by another room. The ceiling of this had been split open by the explosion. Rómulo had run upstairs and down, and he was short of breath.

"Ah, here you are!" he kept repeating.

She said to herself: "When he didn't find me up there, he thought I'd escaped." Rómulo observed that the two books he had brought from the library were there on a table. Through the cover of one he could see the licentious illustrations. He put the *Examples of Monarchies* on the table, too. In the place occupied by the seascape on the upper floor hung a Goya tapestry in very bright yellows, which Rómulo did not like. The duchess, feeling hounded by fate, still refused to lose her composure in front of Rómulo. Rómulo said, disagreeably surprised:

"Oh, there's a telephone here, too."

Glancing away, the duchess asked in a hoarse voice: "Is there any news?"

Rómulo looked at her steadily. The only news there could be was that they had already shot him.

"Yes. He's no longer alive."

Realizing that he ought to say something more, he added:

"Unfortunately."

Still it was not enough. He felt obliged to go on talking and said that the back room had a cracked ceiling and if it rained the water would come through it. Although Her Grace was not using that room because it was beyond the bedroom, it might be unhealthy to have a leaky roof so near. If Her Grace liked—he ended—she could go down to the floor below.

She did not answer. She was looking at the gray mist floating in through one of the windows. It was a gloomy day. The city was beginning to look deserted. The explosions rang lugubriously in the empty streets. The constant artillery fire made going out on the streets a dangerous venture, and there was no safety indoors, either. From time to time a car full of soldiers passed at fantastic speed. Noises mingled confusingly. A motorcycle sounded like a machine gun, and it was impossible to know whether a near-by explosion meant an enemy grenade or a shot from one of the batteries that were being set up in squares and vacant lots.

The duchess had found the French print with the pretty skeleton again and she said to Rómulo: "For heaven's sake, take it away someplace where I can't see it any more." Rómulo fetched the elevator up and got into it with the print. He put it on the floor, lean-

114

ing it against the back wall. He saw that the roses were all half-opened and the buds were giving off a carnal fragrance. He gathered them up and returned to the duchess' rooms. Above the armful of flowers, Rómulo's false grief was reminiscent of a clown's moon-faced solemnity.

"There's some more news, My Lady. Unluckily the house has been invaded."

The duchess was staring "at nothing." Her indifference—thought Rómulo, who could see her in profile—was too great to be true. Rómulo told her what was happening in the park and asked leave to move into a room in the basement with his wife. She said "yes" unhearingly. Rómulo added: "I've managed with some difficulty to keep the soldiers down on the ground floor." Although he expounded the situation in gloomy colors, he did not tell her Lieutenant Ordóñez had been up on the terrace, and kept insisting that he would not fail to warn her if the danger became greater (supposing it really did become so) in time for her to make a decision. Rómulo was still standing with the flowers in his arms, and the duchess did not seem to notice them. He put them in the bathroom and returned to the parlor. The duchess stammered:

"Rómulo, I want to get away from here."

"My Lady," he said, "life in the city's very different. Everything's changed, and you can't move a step without government papers."

The duchess saw there was a hidden pleasure behind whatever Rómulo said. She realized he would do nothing to help her go. She glanced into the open elevator, at the graceful skeleton leaving the ball.

"For heaven's sake, shut that door."

Rómulo obeyed and came back a moment later. The duchess gave him another order:

"Have a look at that window. I don't think it shuts properly."

Rómulo saw that a powerful reflector was fastened to it, one of those that used to be lit on gala nights to illuminate the park. They were lit not only with ornamental intentions but because the King's protection service exacted it. Rómulo saw it was the outer shutters that could not be closed. But the windows shut easily, and with the blinds drawn it would be quite safe. His glance followed the direction of the duchess' eyes, which had lighted on the console, on the white marble top of a console with a gold and mother-of-pearl and steel object lying in the middle of it: the duchess' pistol. Rómulo thought: "She's considering suicide." He could not understand how a woman like the duchess could think of committing suicide for a man like the duke. He came forward solemnly, picked up the weapon, and put it in his pocket.

"Why have you taken it away from me?" she asked.

Rómulo pulled it out and put it back where it was before. The duchess persisted:

116

"If you take that weapon away from me, I'll feel like a prisoner. And I'm not a prisoner, Rómulo. I'm only in hiding."

She asked him, as though it cost her a great effort to do so, if he knew anything about the duke's last moments, and Rómulo thought: "She's in the thick of those last moments."

"No, My Lady, I don't know anything. I only know they've already executed him."

Neither spoke. A tiny butterfly, a moth, was flying in the lighted zone of one of the lamps. Outside the cannon could be heard. The duchess felt a pity that threatened to turn into flooding tears, and she tried so hard to hold back the tears and avoid this that she started laughing. Rómulo's eyes widened in alarm. The duchess kept on laughing and at intervals repeated aloud to herself: "No, no." She insisted she had to get out of the house, out of Madrid, out of Spain. Rómulo said:

"Maybe, if you went with me, we might try to reach a frontier somewhere, Portugal or France."

"Maybe," she said dreamily.

"Her Grace can count on me."

"On you?"

Yet the duchess seemed to be weighing the pros and cons. At last she said:

"They don't trust you."

"I think they do now, My Lady."

The duchess analyzed that "now" and succeeded in

117

giving it the correct meaning. Rómulo told her he had
disconnected the telephone and was going to pull out
the wires in the more visible parts of the tower exten-
sion. And he added:

"Now that Her Grace has no telephone and can't
call me, it'll be understood I can come up any time
during the day or night without being sent for."

She made no reply. Rómulo had turned on his flashlight and for a moment stood looking at the Goya
tapestry. "By the yellow glow of my flashlight," he
was thinking, "this countryside, which isn't countryside, and yet is countryside, seems full of sunshine."
He kept the light shining on the tapestry. The duchess
said nothing, and Rómulo thought he ought to apologize in advance.

"As Her Grace can't call me now. . . ."

She appeared to wake up.

"Very well, but don't ever come here at night after
eleven."

Rómulo went on staring at the tapestry on the wall,
saying to himself: "By the glow of my flashlight, the
countryside's sunny, but the sun's a soft yellow, as
before a storm." He was pleasantly surprised—the
duchess was looking at him and talking to him almost
like a friend—but he thought: "The duchess is calmer
and more confident because the battle's getting tougher
and it looks as though everything'll be over tonight or
tomorrow." He felt obliged to say something contrary
to these hopes.

118

"The war'll go on for a long time My Lady."

"Is that what the soldiers say?" she asked, and added with a tranquillity Rómulo could not understand: "I think it's a question of days."

"The end of the war?"

"At least," she said, glancing at Rómulo in a sinisterly familiar way, "the fall of Madrid."

Rómulo did not want to accept that almost friendly yet sour and gloomy confidence of the duchess. "Perhaps she knows," he was thinking, "about my share in the duke's death and puts up with it as long as she can have me killed some day."

"You don't give my head much time," he said.

The duchess glanced at him, trying to find out what was going on in that head Rómulo considered lost.

"I believe," he added "that when your side gets in they'll at least arrest me, send me to jail."

She seemed to want to probe, too:

"Why?"

"For being trusted by the Reds."

He went on staring into her eyes and saw nothing more than a kind of indifferent confidence in them. He asked:

"Wouldn't Her Grace come to my defense?"

The duchess did not reply. Rómulo, who was seated, stretched his legs out on the carpet and added:

"Or would she leave me in the executioner's hands?"

"When it comes to that, if it really does, we'll see."

119

Shortly afterward, without Rómulo's having spoken again, she said, as so often before:

"It's late, Rómulo."

Rómulo pulled in his legs but did not rise. On the contrary, he said:

"I'm not going. I need to talk to you and know you're listening to me."

The duchess changed color.

"Talk if you want to. As I haven't the courage to jump out the window, I'll have to put up with your being here, and listen to you."

Rómulo began:

"Tonight I only came to see if you felt easy in your mind. I can see you don't. I can see you're not easy in your mind, and I'm sorry. If I could give up my own peace of mind in return for yours. . . ."

Rómulo spread out his legs again. It was like a gesture of proprietorship, of lordliness.

"I've also come, as I was telling you, because I need to talk to you and listen to you. The danger's increasing every day, although we don't like talking about it. Tonight may be the end of everything. Not because the enemy'll come in. It isn't that. The city's better defended every day"—he said this without the least hope of being believed—"but the artillery never stops firing. The planes come over now and then."

The duchess said:

"I know it. I know it the same as you, the same as everybody. And it doesn't matter."

120

Rómulo was not satisfied with that.

"Or perhaps the city'll fall. If the batteries here are increasing by the dozen, they'll be increasing on the other side, too, I say. Those people," he said, pointing in the direction of the cannon, "may get in here. Her Grace believes they'll kill me when Madrid falls. That doesn't matter to me, either. Why should life matter more to me than to His Grace or to Her Grace? . . .

"If Her Grace wants my ruin, and I'm really headed for it since Her Grace wants it, that doesn't stop me from being a happy man. Her Grace will ask: 'Why?' And what am I going to tell Her Grace, since she knows as much about me as I know myself?"

The duchess could bear no more, but she spoke calmly:

"It's true. I know as much as you do. You're a criminal. You're a murderer. Go away."

Rómulo shook his head. "I won't go." With the duchess' words everything had become lighter and easier. She had spoken. And Rómulo had not confessed anything. Rómulo felt almost happy. Nevertheless he was watching the darkened doorway into the bedroom with misgiving. Then he looked at the tapestry. The tapestry was like a window, too. Turning the beam of his flashlight on it, he seemed to be peering into a valley shadowed by the last light of afternoon. The near and distant booming seemed to come from the false horizons of that valley he could see in

121

the tapestry. The air in the tower was cold—Rómulo
thought of the furnaces—and appeared to thicken
into yellow cottonwool around the lamps. Rómulo
said:

"No. Things aren't what they seem."

It was a sentence that, after the duchess' accusations, did not incriminate him. And he added:

"War, fire, blood, what do they matter to us, to you
and me?"

Explosions sounded near by. He was looking at the
tapestry and seeing a low horizon, like that of Cas-
tile. Perhaps the duke lay buried on the other side of
that horizon. He said, pointing to the windows:

"There, out there, things are happening that we
can't understand and don't want to. What do I care
what's happening? Life, what's life? War, blood,
what are they? I don't mean it isn't sad, but over
and above all this I've got my own way to make. A
new way, My Lady."

Rómulo was growing animated:

"I won't say what way it is. Her Grace can say it to
herself if she wants to, because a woman like Her Grace
can do anything in her imagination. I see it plainer
every day. For forty years I've been trying to understand everything going on outside of me and behave
reasonably. Every day I've said yes a dozen times
when maybe I was thinking no. That's what's been my
great foolishness. Or my great crime."

The artillery sounded, and Rómulo added:

"And the foolishness or crime of all those who are firing off cannon now, or being shot at from the other side. Don't you think so?"

The duchess remained silent.

"I don't know what the lives of all those people have been. But from what they're doing now you can figure it out. You can see they're getting back years of making believe they're humble, and there's so much to be gotten back that they have to do it like this: by means of cannon, by means of knives; with blood and fire."

Hearing him, the duchess was thinking: "He's a criminal, but there's a sort of innocence in him. I'm as guilty of the duke's death as he is. And yet at the same time I'm innocent, too. But, if we're all innocent, where does the crime come from? Who hatches it, and where, and what for?" She was looking at Rómulo with animosity, and Rómulo continued:

"I had lots of ideas once, when I was young, that I thought were crazy and tried to get rid of. But they used to come back at night. Later on, by hushing them up, a day came when they didn't return any more. So the years went by. How many? Fifteen? Twenty?"

The duchess was not looking at him, but she heard. And she was thinking: "Rómulo takes life seriously, while I play with it. But life's not the thing Rómulo takes seriously. And it's not the other thing I jeer at, either."

123

"Now I know those crazy ideas were the only ones really worth anything, because instead of coming from my head they came from my blood."

"What ideas, Rómulo?"

Ah, she was listening to him, even though it was in a calculating rather than a friendly way. She wanted to know. She listened to him and did not tell him to be off.

"It isn't easy to explain, but I see it clearly. When people are too unhappy, sometimes they look up at the sky with their teeth clenched in rage or their eyes full of tears. And what do people see up there? A blue vault in the daytime, and at night the stars. The stars, do you hear? And, looking at the stars, people start thinking about getting away from the place they're in and going to some other world, where things are better or different. But do you know what I say, My Lady? That those stars we see are also inhabited, and the people in them sometimes lift up their heads too and look at the sky, just like us. And they look over here, at this star where we live, and dream about everything here being perfect or at least much more beautiful than what they've got."

The duchess said: "Good Lord!" which bewildered Rómulo, as he did not know whether it meant impatience, anguish, or emotion at what she was hearing.

"Those people who dream about us are right. The things that are happening here, the things that are being accomplished now because we've got them in

124

our blood, the things we're getting back—those are the very things they're dreaming about. Everything round us is just as beautiful as they believe it is."

The cannonade was heard again at close quarters. The duchess said with sarcasm:

"That, too? War, too? Death, too?"

Rómulo hesitated before going on, but, lowering his eyes until he seemed to have closed them, he said:

"In those worlds, people dream the same as we do here. There's even somebody dreaming about me. About me and about you. About you and me together. Me talking and you listening to me."

Rómulo had a visionary expression on his face again. The duchess heard him with indifference. She rose, thinking about the innocence and fatality of the crime.

"Yes, Rómulo, everything's splendid and horrible. There's a universal suffering, to which you want to oppose a foolishness that may be universal, too. You see, I've listened to you and understood you, Rómulo. Now go."

Rómulo wavered, but he ended by getting up and going over to the bathroom. He brought out the flowers and began putting them into vases. Then he went to the elevator. As he opened the door, the duchess saw the French print leaning against the Pompeiian ornamentations at the back and shut her eyes. Rómulo noticed and turned the picture round.

From this visit he brought away a curious piece of

evidence. The duchess knew what had happened to the duke, and yet she had not accused him.

He went to the room he had moved into with Balbina, near the *salle d'armes*.

The following morning, the duchess noted in her diary:

"Shortly after Rómulo left last night something incredible happened. Estéban came to the tower. Estéban, the devil. He spent over two hours talking about the duke. He said everything that came into his head, and now I realize that perhaps he talked too much, forgetting it was precisely I who was listening to him. Oh, Lord. Hearing Estéban and accepting what he said without protest, I was only submitting to the universal misery and universal foolishness.

"Estéban jeers at everything. How can you jeer at everything these days? How odd men are. He jeers at everything, and Rómulo admires and reveres everything. It would be just as well to take a lesson from one of them, and for the time being I think I'll take it from Estéban. It's the only thing to do. Who could make me take anything that we're seeing and hearing seriously? God? God, who made the world as it is, God, who tolerates all the horror we know about, and then after tolerating it exacts not only admiration for what He's made but adoration, too? How can you yield to a divinity like that? When I talked about this to Estéban, he said, 'Leave the Lord out of it; He's just as peeved in heaven as we are on earth. Once He sent His Son down here, and after seeing what we did to Him, He took Him back again, all bloodied and jeered at and beaten up and dead, and ever since then He spends His whole time saying: "No, no. It's too much. They played a dirty trick on Me. Those people aren't honest." And when He looks down at the earth He doesn't know what to do about it any more. Maybe one day He thought of sending another member of His family, some distant nephew, but He didn't dare to.' Hearing him talk like that, I laughed.

"When he left, I confess I felt stronger. I believe, as he does, that all the moralizing we do in moments like these is only a mask to cover the physical fear of our flesh. He told me, 'try looking death fearlessly in the face, and you'll see moral and religious feelings aren't necessary.' I think he's right.

"But I can't help asking myself where all this is leading us. He says nowhere. He says nothing leads anywhere. That's true. The idea of having believed you could some day get somewhere by self-respect, kindness, goodness, honor, nobility, etc., etc. seems ridiculous to me now."

That night the ninety-six men of the antitank company arrived, followed by two truckloads of mattresses and blankets. All the soldiers looked very young—about twenty—and had an easy schoolboyish gaiety. The animation was extraordinary and turned the ground floor of the palace and the park into a camp. Some of the boys tried to make fun of Rómulo, but finding him impassive, and realizing they neither offended nor flattered him, they began to leave him alone.

Rómulo went to the garage and found the officers and one of the sergeants there. When Rómulo entered, he realized they were talking about him and what they were saying was not unfavorable. Rómulo thought: "The militiamen are telling them how I gave the duke away." They fell silent in his presence. The officer who always looked bad-tempered—Lieutenant Uriarte —rarely spoke, but he listened to everything that was said without missing a word of it. Lieutenant Ordóñez asked Rómulo the ducal family's name, and he told him all about the titles of both branches and about the mistake of calling the duke "Duke of Arlanza," when that was not his title but his father-in-law's. The lieutenant smiled, listening to him. He gave him a glass of wine, and Rómulo was hesitant about taking it, for he instinctively realized that a little shyness would make their confidence firmer.

Ordóñez had asked each of the militiamen in the guard what his trade was, and, on learning that Ruiz had been a watchmaker, Ordóñez said:

"You don't look like a watchmaker."

Rómulo could not understand how they said "thou" to each other so familiarly when they had only just met. Ordóñez seemed to him a frank fellow with nothing up his sleeve. The other officer worried him more,

128

and when he learned he would be leaving with the company for the front in a few days' time he felt glad. Lieutenant Ordóñez, who was a captain, not a lieutenant—they had promoted him, and he had not yet changed his insignia—was in charge of the school. He had been wounded and was just out of the hospital. The post was considered a quiet billet, and he had been sent here to recuperate.

A corporal came in to say the soldiers preferred to be quartered all together in one room and wanted orders changed to accommodate them. The corporal was mild mannered and shaggy haired.

"He's a Communist," said the captain after he had gone, "and he's got a mania for sticking up notices. If we don't keep a sharp lookout, the house'll be overrun with posters and signboards in less than a week."

One of the sergeants burst out laughing without saying anything, and the captain glanced crossly at him:

"What? He hasn't stuck one up in the sleeping quarters?"

"Two," said the sergeant. "He brought them with him ready-made, on big strips of cloth. There's one that says: 'It's better to die on your feet than live on your knees.' "

The captain clicked his tongue with annoyance.

"All very pretty, but I can't stand that romantic literature. It'll have to come down. Life and death are serious matters to proper men, and they're not talked about in my company. It's unlucky, anyway."

129

He asked Rómulo:

"What about you? Are you a Socialist?"

Rómulo was taken by surprise. Ruiz intervened:

"He's from the same trades-union as me."

"Don't tell me he's a watchmaker, too!"

Outside, the cannon fire sounded more staccato than usual. They were all silent, listening, and Ordóñez said:

"At last we're getting decent artillery."

The captain began speaking seriously:

"The work of these boys we're training is a completely new experience in warfare." The officer added that the soldier, the human factor, was as decisive today as in Hannibal's time, either with machines or without them. Rómulo asked:

"Where are they going to cook the food for the troops?"

"There's a service canteen that'll send a field kitchen round with it every day."

Rómulo breathed more freely.

The next day dawned cold and ashy. Under the gray sky, the cannon seemed to be firing with silencers on them, and the reports sounded muffled. The duchess thought for an instant that her side had broken through the lines and entered the city. She even imagined the commands she heard shouted down below sounded like regular army orders and might be coming from Fascist troops. She peered out of the half-opened win-

dow and among the trees saw a large sign with red
letters painted on a white cloth: "Help the Chinese
soviets." On the window sill she noticed the reflector
again.

It started to drizzle, and the militiamen walking
about the park took shelter in the lodge or the house.
Over fifty volunteers were herded together in Rómulo's
old quarters, waiting for papers drafting them to their
assigned units. Rómulo was wandering in the park
and sought refuge under the marquee at the palace
entrance. The fine gravel there was yellower than ever,
and the gray sky and damp air made it appear more
luminous as well. Several soldiers had taken cover
here, too. Others went past, running through the rain.
Rómulo heard disconnected sentences, loose snatches
of conversation:

"What I say is, I wouldn't get into an armored
truck."

Another voice was singing softly: "Rain, rain, go
away, come again some other day." A corporal swore
laughingly and added:

"D'you think the plating's made of candy?"

A man who looked like a peasant was calling:

"Corporal García!"

The voice woke a small echo at the end of the park
near the washhouse. ". . . García!" Rómulo had
been thinking about the duke too much for the last
three days. He would reconstruct the shooting in his
imagination and linger over small details. "Do they

131

really tie up people's feet when they're going to be shot?" Rómulo felt as though he had tied up the duke's himself. The rain kept on falling softly. The panes of the story-high rectangular marquee, which jutted out like a white vizor above the entrance, flung a halo of pale light over Rómulo and the yellow gravel. And Rómulo, with his hands in his trousers' pockets (an attitude forbidden him in the duke's time), was telling himself that he could go and see the duchess any time "before eleven."

Night came down dark and moonless. A little before nine o'clock, as Rómulo was crossing the park, he was flung to the ground by a string of explosions. It was as if the sky had been torn to shreds above him. He remained on the ground for a few seconds, heard the planes fly away, and when he got up he saw half the park wreathed in a dense cloud of smoke and dust. Just before the explosions the reflector in the tower window had flashed on. It lit up Rómulo's house, the park, the flag on the roof. The reflector had gone out just as the explosions occurred, perhaps broken. "But," thought Rómulo, "one of the militiamen may have seen that reflector, like I did." From the place where Rómulo's lodgings had been a moment before, cries of pain were now issuing. He went to the palace to fetch the officers, who had retired to the cellars with the soldiers when the sirens had given the alarm. On the way he noticed that all the glass in the ground-floor windows was smashed and saw shrapnel marks on the front door, which also had two deep cracks in its stone arches. A slight breeze was tugging at the cloud of smoke and dust which shrouded the park and wafting it away toward the center of the city.

The officers, the soldiers, and Rómulo walked over to the park gates, which had been wrenched from their hinges. Beside them they saw Rómulo's house turned into a heap of ruins. Smoke was rising from the rubble, dense and foul-smelling smoke. The militiaman who had been on sentry duty at the time of the explosion was Estradera, and he approached them with his face covered with blood. Pointing to the tower, he said:

"They sent down 'a stream' of light from over there."

As soon as Estradera had said it, he fell unconscious to the ground. Captain Ordóñez had heard him. They carried the wounded man away to the nearest hospital. The captain, seeing the soldiers getting in among the ruins, said:

"Be careful, there may be live bombs about."

The first casualty they pulled out of the rubble told them the planes had thrown down flares before dropping the bombs. Rómulo clutched at this new version and said he had seen the flares, too. They all appeared to accept the flares as a natural and possible fact. The wounded man said there must be about fifty people trapped in the ruins. Rómulo could never have imagined his wife's dead body would be found among

133

them. She was mangled, her face and hair burned, and when he tried to lift her up she bent about all over, as though she had no bones. Rómulo heard voices round him but he was alone in front of that body, with his flashlight turned on. A soldier tried to lead him away, but Rómulo refused to go. Between him and Balbina's body his stare hung coagulated in the dense night air stabbed by criss-cross beams from other electric flashlights. Rómulo was saying senseless words, with the duchess' image in his mind and Estradera's voice in his ears: "A stream of light came from the tower." He had seen it as plainly as the sentry. The captain told him to call up the district first-aid station and ask for ambulances, and Rómulo went to the telephone.

When he returned to the park he could not find the the captain. He searched for him everywhere in vain. He was afraid of coming upon his wife's body again. He saw a disorderly scurry in the park and retreated into the palace once more, groped for an armchair in the dark, and sank down into it. The possibility of seeing Balbina's burned face again, with her smoldering hair, terrified him. In the stillness of the armchair his emotions seemed to be crowding up on him until they overwhelmed him, but, perhaps as a natural defense of his nerves, a drowsiness stronger than his terror stole over him, and he fell asleep.

Half an hour later the cold woke him up. He rose, numbed. In the kitchen a group of soldiers were making coffee. From the park came the humming of the ambulance engine. Rómulo said hopefully to himself: "Perhaps they'll take that poor body away before I come out." Now and then a flash from the headlamps shone through the broken panes, and as they were turned quickly on and off to find the way in the dark they seemed like silent explosions. He heard Captain Ordóñez being called. The soldiers were peering into the hall and vainly yelling his name. Rómulo said to himself unawares: "Everything in life is nothing." But life was a jumble of vice-versas, and the contrary could also be said. Anything, the most insignificant thing, is everything in life. He tried to explain his indifference in the face of the catastrophe by thinking that the planes might return at any moment, and the danger in which he himself still was, made him take the death of Balbina and the others rather lightly.

He needed to go to the tower as soon as possible, but the commotion in the park was increasing, and he dared not get far away. Besides, the duchess had forbidden him to come up after eleven. And it would not be easy to face the duchess. But Rómulo told himself: "I'll go when the confusion dies down a bit." He tried unsuccessfully to explain to himself what had occurred in the tower for the reflector to have lit up the way it did, and seemed to solve it all in the following conclusion: "With or without the light, the same thing would have happened." He had Balbina's image constantly on his mind, although he was not thinking about her. "Tonight they didn't cut off the

135

electricity when they heard the sirens." If they had
cut it off, the reflector could not have been lit, and in
that case the enemy would not have seen the Republican flag floating over the lodge; perhaps they might
not have identified it as the district's seventeenth recruiting office. Although it was not necessary for them
to know it was a military establishment in order to
bomb it.

But suppose the reflector was the cause of everything; then somebody had turned it on. And Rómulo
wondered: "Could the duchess have done that? And
why?" He could not go on thinking, because Balbina's
body got in his way, and he raised his chest a little to
breathe better and told himself: "Perhaps poor Balbina didn't realize. . . . She didn't suffer."

He went out into the park. They had pulled twenty-
eight corpses out of the ruins and were still working.
The soldiers kept repeating the number in pained
amazement. They worked in darkness, glancing up at
the sky from time to time with distrustful calm.
Rómulo asked after Estradera and was told he was
still at the hospital, but his wounds were slight and of
no consequence. One of the soldiers joked: "It looks
as though that comrade's got a hard head."

Not long afterward, Estradera returned with his
head bandaged. Rómulo asked him where he had seen
the light in the park coming from, but he, realizing
there were discrepancies and that perhaps he was not
quite sure himself whether it had been a reflector or

flares, shrugged his shoulders. When Rómulo saw that most of the dead and wounded—his wife among the first—had been evacuated, he went toward the tower. The nearer he got the more alarmed he felt, without knowing why. He could not imagine any concrete danger, yet he made sure his pistol was in working order when he noticed that the hanging covering the staircase entrance had been wrenched away at one corner. Reaching the door, he heard murmurs inside. He rushed in.

The duchess was standing in the middle of the room. Following the direction of her eyes, Rómulo found Captain Ordóñez lying on the floor almost behind the door, breathing with difficulty and trying fumblingly to rise. One whole side of his face was covered with blood. The duchess said in an impassive voice:

"Be careful, Rómulo."

Rómulo looked at the duchess and then at the wounded man. She went on speaking in too calm a voice for her serenity to have been real.

"Perhaps he's going to shout. He can still get up. And he's got a weapon."

Rómulo bent over the wounded man, who appeared unaware of things. The captain's arm trailed at his side, and he was doing nothing to defend himself. Rómulo went down on one knee and tried to raise him.

"Captain Ordóñez. . . ."

At the same time he heard the duchess speaking:

"I didn't shoot him, Rómulo."

137

The duchess spoke coldly, not at all in the grieved tone of a person apologizing. Rómulo said to himself: "Well, if it wasn't her, who was it?" He glanced at the bedroom door with the feeling there was somebody in there. Surprise prevented him from co-ordinating his thoughts and actions. He did not know where to turn. The captain raised his head and stared at Rómulo without recognizing him. He put a hand to his temple and scratched at the wound, and the blood flowed out in greater quantities. The wounded man fell back again, and Rómulo held him compassionately in his arms. Lowering her voice, the duchess repeated:

"Don't trust him, Rómulo. Take his weapons away."

Rómulo laid the wounded man on the carpet, put a cushion under his head, and glanced about. He saw an empty shell from a pistol on the floor, picked it up, and noted at a glance that it was of much larger caliber than the duchess' weapon. "If I went into the bedroom now, the same thing would certainly happen to me as happened to the captain." And he felt an irresistible inclination to go in. But he went to the bathroom to fetch a towel.

A painful discouragement slowed his steps and the movements of his hands. "There's another man, another one who comes at night the way the duke used to." He did not know where this unknown man was hidden or from what quarter the attack might come. He found nobody in the bathroom. He moistened a towel and came back to the wounded officer. He saw

138

that the latter had changed his position, was lying face downward, and no longer seemed to be breathing. Rómulo turned him gently over onto his back and said to the duchess:

"I think he's not alive any more."

"Are you sure?"

Rómulo put his hand on the captain's heart; then he laid his ear against it.

"He's dead."

The duchess said in a voice of entreaty:

"Then, Rómulo, please get him out of here. He's been bleeding there for over three hours."

Without answering, Rómulo started to obey her. He noticed that the flowers in the vases were gleaming just as he had thought they would. Rómulo did not quite see how he was to get the body away. The sirens were wailing again. Rómulo thought of the elevator, then the park.

The sirens kept on. "If I go out with his body over my shoulder, they'll see me. They'll be sure to see me." There is always a man watching anyone who tries to spirit a corpse away. Perhaps the air raid would help him. "The man who might see me will be hiding somewhere during the bombardment, to escape the bombs." Since the alarms did not generally last very long, he made ready to take full advantage of the time. The first antiaircraft guns went off. In the midst of that already familiar booming, he picked up the corpse, hoisted it over his shoulder, and went toward the elevator door. He saw the duchess darting about looking for something and stopped. She said harshly to him:

"Those stains will have to be cleaned up."

There were smears of blood on the carpet. She picked up the same towel Rómulo had fetched from the bathroom and put it down again. Without knowing what to do, she took a bunch of flowers out of a vase and tried, first with the asparagus ferns around them and later with the whole bunch, to suppress the terrible evidence. Rómulo told her, entering the elevator:

"Leave it. I'll do it."

But she kept on nervously without hearing him. Rómulo heard a little sob and glanced back. It was not the duchess. He would have liked it to have been her, but the duchess was no longer there. It was the body of the captain, whose thoracic cavity, compressed against the gardener's shoulder, had emitted the air from the lungs.

The elevator started going down and then stopped suddenly between the first and second floors. They had cut off the electricity. Rómulo stood waiting in the dark for the alarm to finish and the current to be switched on again. After waiting a long time he put the captain's body carefully on the floor and sat down.

Rómulo was in the elevator, in the same position, all night and nearly all the following day. By some incomprehensible chance they did not turn the electricity on again, and Rómulo remained penned up for almost twenty hours, thinking: "The man who's done all this is upstairs. He's still there with the duchess. Who is he? And why does she let him come and bloody her carpets and scatter death from her window?" He tried to remember all the duchess' family connections, and among them found young men who had never seemed to him capable of doing things like that. "On the contrary, you would have said they were as gentle as women." He knew he would get no inkling of the man who had stayed upstairs. He recalled the little pistol with its gold and mother-of-pearl mountings, recalled the yellow light on the carpet, recalled the captain's body as though it were not there in front of him. He also recalled the licentious illustrations in those sumptuously bound books. He recalled everything except Balbina's mangled body.

He could not manage to picture the duchess' visitor, but he repeated to himself time and again: "He's upstairs with the duchess, and I'm shut in here with his victim. Shut in with a dead body." For the captain had ceased to be "Captain Ordóñez" and become "a dead body." Yet he could still hear the captain's last words at the park gates after the bombardment: "Be careful, there may be some live bombs in the rubble." Rómulo was hungry and thirsty, above all thirsty.

Late in the day the light suddenly came on, and the elevator started down again. When it stopped at the bottom with a soft thud, Rómulo heard voices and did not dare step out. "If I had any luck," he told himself,

141

"there'd be another bombardment somewhere near the palace tonight, and then everything would be easier." For he realized he ought not to try to come out until nightfall.

The bombardment began before eleven o'clock. In the confusion, things were just as Rómulo had hoped. When he went across the park with the corpse over his shoulder, the bombardment was at its height. "If they drop too near," he thought, "this poor man's body may serve to protect me." But, when he reached the furnaces and went to throw the corpse into the fire, he had a suspicion. Perhaps the mysterious visitor had been the captain himself, and, due to a series of circumstances beyond his understanding, he had finally come to die at the duchess' hands. Rómulo forgot certain details that would easily have proved this impossible. He made ready to throw the body into the furnace. The fire was not hot enough. He left the body on the ground, shoveled on more coal, and opened the dampers as far as possible. A draught immediately shot up, and, when the fire seemed to have revived, he picked up the body again from the ground and with great difficulty heaved it in. It spread out as it fell and lay stretched along the whole bank of glowing coals. Rómulo threw several more shovelfuls over it and then closed the top opening as well as he could with the metal hatch. He used his foot to deaden the slam and pulled it away badly bruised.

As he was about to leave, he noticed the corpse had

142

lost one of its shoes. Just then Rómulo remembered that masculine footprints sometimes appeared on the carpet in the duchess' rooms, and it occurred to him to keep the shoe and compare it—if he had a chance —with those marks. Although the decision seemed stupid to him as soon as he had made it, he took the shoe along with him without knowing why.

"I was shut up in the elevator for nearly twenty-four hours, and the soldiers must have noticed that I was missing." The lapse was either too long or too short to justify his absence. "I can say I went to make some arrangements about poor Balbina's body." He never thought of his wife, but under everything he said and did she was present. He did not want to think of her, because that broken image with its burning hair hurt him too much. He went to the kitchen for a drink of water; after drinking the second glass, he broke into abundant perspiration and went on up to the tower. Before entering the duchess' rooms he left the captain's shoe on the stairs, for his suspicion appeared groundless to him, and any verification ridiculous.

The duchess was not there. Seeing the flowers smashed and scattered on the carpet, Romulo thought: "The bloodstains were enough to drive her away from here. She must be on the third floor." He went down and tripped over the shoe in the dark. He picked it up and, before going into the third-floor rooms, threw it away again and heard it rolling down the flight that

143

led to the second floor. The rooms were arranged in the same formation but were furnished differently. Red and yellow tones predominated, and a Zurbarán hung where the Goya tapestry was. It was a somber picture, showing a saint with a face like a hanged man against a beguilingly simple background. At the saint's feet lay a skull that seemed to glimmer in the shadows. The curtains in these rooms had the ducal coronet on them, and the chairs and divans were fussily upholstered.

"I don't like these rooms," the duchess said. "The idea of being so near my mother's apartment upsets me."

Rómulo thought: "She is talking to me as if nothing had happened."

"Come down to the basement," he proposed, "next to the *salle d'armes*."

"Are you living there with Balbina?"

Rómulo looked straight at her without answering. She did not understand. In Rómulo's eyes she saw something like an immense recrimination.

"Balbina!" said Rómulo gravely, and he smiled with bitterness.

The duchess seemed to realize.

"Rómulo, I'm not to blame. But anyway I ask you to forgive those who may be. To forgive them for my sake."

He noticed a nervous hardness in her tone. "She is talking differently," he said to himself, "and she herself seems like somebody else." With a grave expression he said aloud:

"It's the dead that'll have to forgive them."

From the park came the smell of dust, gunpowder, and smoke.

"It was Balbina's death that most affected all of them. Maybe you don't know it, but poor Balbina spent her whole time weeping and praying for you."

The duchess' indifference remained unshaken, and she asked him with a queer humor:

"Are you still in the best of worlds?"

Rómulo felt this was difficult to answer, but he said: "Yes, My Lady."

The duchess became full of cold aggressive curiosity:

"If that is so, Rómulo, you aren't feeling your wife's death."

Rómulo thought he had not understood.

"I'm not feeling it?"

"I dare you to tell the truth," the duchess insisted. "Me?"

Seeing he was completely bewildered, the duchess added:

"Inside you there's something that's remained cold and indifferent to your wife's death."

The duchess was implacable. In the shadows of the room her eyes seemed afire.

"And deeper down still, deeper yet inside you, there's something that rejoices."

145

Rómulo could not say anything. The duchess' words were so unexpected. The duchess added, murmuring to herself:

"There's universal pain and there's universal foolishness, but there's also universal meanness."

Rómulo said at length:

"I think Her Grace is mistaken."

She went on:

"You'd been married for over ten years."

"Sixteen years, My Lady," Rómulo amended, very pale.

The duchess seemed very talkative, and this surprised Rómulo as much as the meaning of the words she spoke to him:

"You were bound to Balbina by everyday habit. And only by habit, nothing more. Living with her without loving her was sometimes uphill work, eh?"

The duchess did not take her eyes off him. Distant voices were heard. Soldiers working in the ruins. And she went on:

"Sixteen years of living with her, that is, not living at all. Sixteen years of your life lost."

"Lost?" he asked, unable to comprehend the duchess' change of character and trying to explain the reasons to himself. She continued talking:

"Yes. The best years of your life. All your youth. But now things are different. It isn't that you're glad of her death for its own sake."

146

The duchess paused, but Rómulo said nothing. She continued:

"It's not that. I know you're incapable of wishing her any ill, and, if it had been in your power to prevent what happened, you'd have done so at the risk of your own life."

"That's true," he said, calmer.

Returning to the hard tone of her first words, the duchess added:

"She's dead, and everything's different now. She isn't what she was. Faced with your dead wife, you find to your surprise that you can not only respect her but maybe even regard her as a superior being."

Rómulo's anxiety changed to misgiving and alarm. What was wrong with the duchess? She went on:

"Now those sixteen years of your life haven't been lost. Now you haven't made the bad bargain of losing the best part of your youth. That time's ennobled, and everything about it is taking on new value. Then you realize that, besides your natural sorrow for Balbina's death, you have a right to a certain feeling of happiness."

Rómulo appeared disconcerted. In the shadows of the room there were acute angles. She was "somebody else." And she was saying:

"I know it's true, and you needn't feel ashamed of it."

Listening to her, Rómulo said to himself: "She is talking to me like this because she feels guilty. She needs to talk so much and to say extravagant things because she has a lover." This idea made the blood come up to his throat. He was also thinking that, if the duchess was telling him all this, she must have felt the same herself about the duke's death. But the duchess would not allow him to enter those depths of her soul.

"If it's the way you say, then there's nothing wrong in it."

"No, Rómulo."

He said aloud to himself:

"Yet these days I'm beginning to realize there's always something fond and loving behind even the most horrible things, something stronger and higher that saves us. I mean, even if there was something wrong in it, that evil would never have the last word."

The duchess kept on, smiling:

"No. There's always a greater evil. And after the most horrible evil we can imagine, there's no loving reason at all, only a huge roar of laughter."

"Who laughs?"

"God."

Rómulo denied it. He insisted on his "loving reason that saves everything," and the duchess pretended not to understand. Rómulo said:

"For instance, when I came here after the bombardment, I didn't realize anything of what you've just said. I was thinking about what I'd seen down below. I mean, when I came here the day before yesterday.

And even then I found the captain lying on the carpet when I came in. But it isn't necessary to repeat how things happened. You know, and it's enough for me that you know. I came in and saw you. And I saw that sunny valley in the tapestry, the one that's upstairs. And everything changed, everything was different. The blood, the frightfulness and misery in the park, all disappeared."

"Oh, now I see. . . . Then you understand how you can be glad of Balbina's death?"

He hesitated. Those words were still too strong; they surprised him, and he would never get used to them. But he said:

"Even if I understood it, My Lady, there are other things I'll never understand as long as I live."

"What do you mean?"

"I mean I'll never understand why you still have people around you who're bent on getting you killed."

The duchess said nothing, and Rómulo went on:

"If it was only a matter of saving you from the risk of the Reds, I know it would all be easy, but every time I come to the tower I feel much greater dangers in the air. How am I to save you from them? How am I to save you from your friends?"

The duchess returned to her indifference.

"If I want to risk my life, there's only one thing for you to do: bow your head and keep quiet. If you don't like that, you can denounce me to your fellows."

"She doesn't value my protection at all, and she

149

wouldn't value anybody's," thought Rómulo. From time to time, worried about whether the corpse he had flung into the furnace was being properly consumed, he put his hand on the radiator. Whenever he did so he wore an expression of secret doubt. The duchess watched him nervously. After feeling the radiator for the fourth time, Rómulo made an oblique gesture and said:

"Just as we hang onto our warmth while living, the poor dead hang onto their cold."

He laid his hand on the radiator again. The duchess avoided looking at him, and Rómulo said:

"My Lady, you must make up your mind to leave these tower rooms at once. Come down to the basement, where the windows aren't broken. Or go up to the attics where they'll never find you. There's a fairly comfortable place there, where the main steam pipe goes through."

And, as the duchess said nothing, Rómulo thought to encourage her by saying:

"Be reasonable, My Lady."

Neither the basement rooms nor the attics communicated with the street. The duchess knew this quite well.

"There's a great difference," she said, "in our way of seeing reason."

Seeing him rise and approach her, the duchess glanced at the mother-of-pearl pistol on the console and seemed to be measuring the distance that sepa-

rated her from it. Rómulo went over to the table,
quietly picked up the weapon, and put it in his pocket.
Beneath his calm were strained nerves, and in his eyes
the violence of that danger imperfectly seen, and of
that weapon, shone. "She has a lover," he said to himself, exasperated.

"Only in your being a woman. A woman," he repeated, lowering his voice. "I know that woman. I've
seen her. The man's seen her and kept the sight of her
in his eyes forever. Through his eyes she's gone into
the marrow of his bones, that woman. He has her with
him always, awake or asleep. With all she is or thinks.
With all she says or doesn't say. Just as she is. I've
seen her, and I'm seeing her now. I, I, a man. Yes, a
man, I. When I'm naked I'm a man, the same as Her
Grace is a woman. I go to the swimming pool and
undress, and if I wanted to swim I would. And I read
that book about the King and the Queen. Inside me,
I'm a man. In my mind, in my will, in my blood, I'm
a man. Can't you see me, eh? Look at me carefully,
if you haven't seen me. Look at me as a man and not
a ghost. And look at me like what you are: like a
woman."

Rómulo came nearer, and she drew back.

"I'm not a woman, Rómulo."

Rómulo repeated to himself: "She has a lover." He
stretched out his hand and, taking her by the shoulder,
ripped her coat off with a single jerk of his arm. The
duchess emerged from the fur coat naked to the waist.

151

She was wearing a pair of blue pajama trousers, but her breasts and back were bare. Rómulo kept the coat in his hand and walked forward, dragging it along. The duchess crossed her arms over her chest. Rómulo said, taking this modesty as a tribute:

"If you're not a woman, why do you cover yourself up? Don't cover yourself. I've seen you already. Why are you covering yourself now when you didn't the other day?"

He was still advancing, and she was retreating. She let fall her arms. She looked like an ivory idol. Rómulo blinked with disappointment, but, staring at her uncovered breasts and wounded by her lack of modesty, he said:

"Yes. That's better. I've seen your body before, and from it—from this flesh, and these eyes that are frightened now and were mocking a moment ago—comes the light that makes everything more beautiful here than in other worlds. In those worlds they dream of us. Of you and me. They dream of me, too. Of me, seeing you naked now."

Rómulo gazed at her with shining eyes, and his voice shook. She stammered:

"I'm cold."

"Can't you feel my eyes burning your skin like live coals? Aren't my eyes a man's eyes, by any chance? Is that why you aren't covering yourself with your hands as you did before?"

The duchess appeared to be trembling. Once or

152

twice she made a gesture as though to cover herself up, but she went on standing there with her bare breasts, looking Rómulo in the eyes coldly, expressionlessly. Rómulo saw only a statue in her. And he saw her confusedly. He went toward her or drew back from her—he could not have said exactly whether he approached or retreated—stumbling against a lamp and the corner of a piece of furniture.

"Aren't my eyes burning you?" he repeated. Doesn't the heat of my blood reach you?"

She said nothing. She looked at him, heard him, and did not answer. Rómulo threw the coat at her. She put it on, buried her head in the furs, sank onto a divan, and closed her eyes. Rómulo said in a hoarse voice:

"But, if they dream about us and adore us, we have to deserve it by being really what we are. You a woman. I a man. Being it completely and to the very end."

She was not looking at him. Neither did she seem to be listening to him. After a long while in silence, Rómulo began wondering if she had fallen asleep—her head was lowered and her eyes shut. Rómulo murmured more composedly:

"Look at me. Or at least listen to me. All the danger, all the insecurity comes from just one thing: because Her Grace won't listen to me. If suspicions gather round what the sentry said about 'a stream of light,' Her Grace is lost. They'll kill her. And, if they

153

kill her, the whole world—do you hear, My Lady?—
the whole world'll be lost, too."

He grew excited again. She smiled with her eyes
and lips. Rómulo could not understand it. The duchess
was here, but that smile took her far away. In her
imagination she was seeing other things and laughing
about those things in her imagination, which Rómulo
could not reach. But she spoke:

"We're all lost. What of it?"

Rómulo glanced at the lamp in the center of the
room, which had at its three corners silver figures
shaped like mermaids, with firm, erect breasts, and
saw the light shining on their metal curves as it had
shone on the duchess' breasts. Rómulo thought, breathing with difficulty: "She's right. I always have been
lost. Sixteen years of my life lost. The best part of my
youth. Maybe everybody loses their youth, that is,
their life. But some of us get it back. This doesn't
mean that, when I heard that voice twenty years ago
and wouldn't listen to it, I wasn't committing a great
crime, the greatest of crimes." What Rómulo said to
the duchess was:

"I would like to ask you a question."

She did not answer. Rómulo, seeing her mute and
sad, felt ashamed of his violence. But he insisted:

"I would like to know who it was murdered the
captain."

The duchess made no reply. After a long silence
she said:

154

"How horrible to have to stay on here!"

Really, everything for forty-eight hours had seemed to be gradually invaded by the larvae of madness. Rómulo said:

"If you want to get away from Madrid and Spain, think about what can be done and count on me. We'll go together.".

"No. Not that."

"Then you shall go alone."

The duchess shook her head:

"I don't think you'll do anything to help me get away from here."

Rómulo heard once more the voices of his youth. Listening to them, he touched the radiator again, calculating from the heat whether the incineration was proceeding or not. Rómulo said:

"Nothing in the world matters so much to me as My Lady's safety. That's why I feel I've a right to ask her something. To ask her something as man to woman."

"As man to woman?"

"Yes."

The duchess said:

"But that isn't possible."

Rómulo turned pale.

He was going to ask something in a bitter tone, but just as he spoke he changed his words:

"If you're not a woman, what are you?"

"I? You've said it already. I'm a dream."

Rómulo came nearer. She got up again with a movement of alarm. Rómulo took her by the waist and pressed her violently against him. He could feel her struggling between his chest and arm, but with less strength than he used in holding her there. She could not escape unless he wanted to release her. It was the first time he had felt her against his body since that day she had wanted to shout "her truth" from the window.

"A dream?" said Rómulo.

She saw his eyes had yellow lights in them like a cat's.

"Let go of me, Rómulo."

"A dream?"

"Rómulo!" she cried desperately, glancing toward the bedroom door. "We're not alone."

Rómulo released her, looking in the same direction. He could see nobody. The duchess had drawn away from him. Rómulo went toward her with his hands in the air like a blind man.

"If we are not alone, who is the other?"

He stopped as he passed near the bedroom door. He wanted to go and see who was in there, supposing anybody really was, but a confused feeling of respect for the duchess' private life held him back. He sat down on the divan and spoke while staring at the bedroom door.

"If we're not alone, it means there's somebody in there. Who is it?"

He sat silent, thinking: "Whoever it is doesn't de-

156

serve to be in there, because he can hear me and hasn't said a word. Because he knows I've undressed her, held her in my arms, and he hasn't said anything." He listened. Nothing could be heard. The duchess had sat down, closed her eyes, and buried her head in the furs again, thinking: "It isn't his fault." Rómulo wanted to go into the bedroom, but he realized it was "her bedroom" and could not make up his mind to do it. That respect—he thought all at once—was only a way of fencing him in with reasons. And he wanted to be faithful to the Rómulo of his youth. He rose and went into the bedroom, which was in darkness. He walked to and fro opening cupboards, and then she heard him opening the door to the other room and entering it. His hurry was aggressively intent. The duchess watched him tranquilly from the doorway. Rómulo came back:

"Where's the man who lit the reflector? Where is he? The man who killed the captain."

She kept silent. Rómulo came nearer:

"Where's that man, the one who comes to sleep with you at night?"

The duchess turned pale, her eyes blazing and her teeth clenched with rage. She looked stronger than everything around her. She seemed to give up her own indignation and exclaimed:

"You can't help being what you are!"

"Me . . . ? Who am I?"

"You know."

"Yes. I know. I am a man."

She was silent. Rómulo gazed at her with a mute anxiety, but she did not speak. Rómulo repeated his words, but now in a depressed and timid tone:

"A man."

It seemed as if the duchess was going to speak, but she said nothing. Apparently very tired, she sat down and hid her face in her hands. Rómulo thought she was weeping. If she was weeping, Rómulo could not keep on being hard or aggressive.

"Forgive me, My Lady."

Sometimes Rómulo used the servants' form of address—the third person—when speaking with her and occasionally the familiar "you." She uncovered her face so that Rómulo could see she was not weeping.

"You're crazy, Rómulo."

Rómulo asserted:

"But maybe not as crazy as you'd like. Weren't you trying to convince me I was glad of Balbina's death? Don't you want me to laugh at yesterday's catastrophe? Don't you want me to think it's funny I stayed shut up in that elevator for twenty-four hours with a dead body? Isn't that what you want? And isn't that madness?"

Fearing Rómulo would get wrought up again, the duchess spoke in a persuasive voice:

"Rómulo, I'm not asking that of you."

"Well, what are you asking of me?"

"To be stronger than all the madness around us."

Rómulo gazed at her without speaking.

"Why?" he asked after a long silence.

"You know I need your help."

"Am I not useful enough for your needs?"

"No."

"What more can I do?"

She spoke with an almost friendly softness.

"Rómulo, you see what's happening. Violence and crime are already closing in on us forever, and I need you quiet, serene, capable of saving yourself and saving me."

Rómulo smiled without speaking. He looked at the Zurbarán picture, seeing that saint with the ecstatic expression and then contemplating the skull at his feet —a skull with open mouth that seemed to be singing—not knowing what to say.

The duchess, seeing him hesitate, added, raising her voice and looking him in the face:

"Go and see to the heating. Go and see that everything's in order. If any clues are left around, they'll find out about you, they'll know at once it was you."

She was speaking as though Rómulo had been guilty of the captain's death. In case there was any doubt, she added:

"That murder would cost you pretty dear."

"Me?"

"Yes, you."

Rómulo tried to smile:

"But it wasn't I."

"That doesn't settle anything. The crime's there. Somebody committed it."

"Yes. Somebody committed it. Who?"

The duchess glanced at him in surprise:

"I hope you're not going to accuse me of it."

Rómulo could not understand.

"I'm willing to offer my head in place of Her Grace's, if it comes to losing it. But I won't offer it for anybody else's."

The duchess said with an indolent gesture:

"The blame's all mine."

Rómulo denied it:

"It's not true. It can't be true."

"It *is* true, Rómulo; but, anyhow, what does it matter? Get along and keep on being faithful to your dream. Isn't there a reason higher than all this blood, all these ruins?"

"I think so."

"Well, get along and do your duty."

Rómulo said to himself: "Maybe after what's happened the lover won't come back any more." The duchess kept ordering him to leave with her glance, and he started to go, thinking: "There are no flowers in these rooms. The flowers were left upstairs. They were scattered about and crushed on the carpet and some of them bloodstained. They were like the captain's funeral flowers." He focused his flashlight on the Zurbarán painting, in the lower part of which the skull continued singing. Realizing that it was nearly

160

morning and he must leave the palace before dawn, so as to telephone from somewhere or other and justify his absence, he went slowly down and on the stairs tripped so thoroughly over the captain's shoe that he nearly fell.

From the duchess' diary:

"When Estéban put out the lights in the room last night, opened the window, and turned on the reflector —to revenge the duke's death, according to what he told me—I said to him: 'Are you crazy?' He kissed me without answering. 'They're going to fire at us, they're going to kill us.' He laughed at the danger and said: 'In whatever we do, there are always risks and threats, that's something nobody can get away from.' The fact of our being in the same danger as the militiamen made me accept it all more easily. For a moment it gave me a feeling of suicide, as though I were about to crumble, standing among the ruins of my own house.

"Afterward that poor captain came. That was still worse. I had him there in front of me for hours and hours until. . . .

"Satan slept upstairs on the fourth floor. He's gone, but he'll be back.

"I'm right in the middle of the whirlwind, and it's swirling tighter round me every minute. What am I to do? He tells me just what I told my husband: you've got to know how to lose.

"But he tells me lots of other things about cruelty, and the divine nature of cruelty, which I daren't write down.

"The fact is, there's some truth in all this, and I ought rightly to shrink from a man of his sort, yet the more atrocities he piles up the more I feel something like admiration and confidence growing in me."

The duchess stopped writing and started exploring these new rooms that were unfamiliar to her. On a table with the other two books she saw the one about *Examples of Monarchies*. She went on searching. In one of the cupboards, she found a big bundle of cloth. It was an old fire-colored garment, rolled up to show a green lining like a vestment. It made a voluminous bundle on which the duchess' glance at first rested absent-mindedly. "Rómulo would 'offer his head' for me, but not for Estéban, according to what he says. But isn't it the same thing?" She was opening out the folds of cloth. "It's the green robe." They called it "the green robe" without knowing why. It was the habit of a now vanished order of chivalry. And as she unrolled it, a kind of brocaded tablecloth, used for taking Communion in bed in case of sickness, fell out onto the floor. There also fell out of the same green robe, as though it were giving birth to them, a merry band of Punch-and-Judy puppets. The dolls spilled over the floor, striking the oddest attitudes. An old butler had been accustomed to make puppet shows with them for the duchess when she was a child. "If

Rómulo's already lost his head, what can it matter whether he offers it for one of us or the other?"

There were all kinds of dolls. Soldiers, frock-coated gentlemen, peasants, princesses, queens, village girls could be found among them. There was also a judge. Some had fallen in comic positions, with their arms spread out or stretched up.

The duchess began sitting them against the back of the divan. When they were all there, she looked at them ironically and said:

"Why should they have turned up, here and now?"

It was like an act of magic. Of that magic which surrounded her. Though certainly Rómulo, in his refusal to accept all responsibilities, seemed to be escaping from the magic circle in which she held him. Looking at the judge, she remembered: "The butler we had when I was a child had studied for the priesthood, and sometimes he used to put in bits of Latin. He would make the judge say, when the show ended: '*Acta est fabula.*'" The duchess picked up another doll: the Queen. She recalled how the butler made his voice grotesque by putting a little metal tube in his mouth, as wandering peddlers do at children's fairgrounds.

The duchess replaced the green robe in the cupboard, but she left the puppets out. She looked at them all and thought rather sadly: "It's like a law court."

There was a queen with a crown, Queen Hypotenuse. And the duchess, remembering the *Booke of the*

Examples of Monarchies, which she had on the table and read frequently, repeated to herself: "Man is king. The queen is man's illusion. Together the two of them form the monarchy that rules over the universe." And thinking of that symbolical king she materialized him in Rómulo and not in Estéban. Rómulo was the King. She was the Queen. "I am the Queen, ideal ambition." She was about to laugh, but she saw Queen Hypotenuse smiling, leaning her grotesque head against the back of the divan, and she became suddenly grave.

CHAPTER
FOUR

RÓMULO LEFT THE HOUSE BY THE SAME GATE
where he had one night lain in wait for the duke
in the darkness. The silence and the solitude
of the streets gave him a sinister feeling. The first
thing he noticed was that the farther away he went,
the nearer he seemed to be to the palace and its problems. He roamed about the deserted streets until dawn.
Then he saw an open pharmacy and went into it
and called the palace on the telephone. A sergeant
answered. Rómulo asked him whether he had been
needed during the time he was away and explained
the reasons for his absence just as he had planned.
"Next time I have to go out," he said in the voice of
somebody regretting something, "I'll leave them the
keys." The sergeant reassured him and asked after
Captain Ordóñez. Rómulo pretended to be surprised.

"Wasn't he sent to the front?"

The sergeant knew nothing. Rómulo said he had heard him mention something about being sent to the front soon.

Shortly afterward, heading for the viaduct by which he thought of going down to the Calle de Segovia, he saw a little garden behind some iron railings with a marble statue of Venus in the middle of it, covering her breasts with her arms. Rómulo smiled as he looked at her.

It was eight o'clock by the time he reached home, and the soldiers of the antitank company had started work. He went straight down to the basement. Once in his room, he lay on the bed thinking he had forgotten every depressing aspect of his position. He could hear the battle in the distaance. "At this very moment, a soldier's falling." To Rómulo, falling meant being left as Balbina had been left, with legs bending about in all directions and hair on fire. "At this very instant, dozens of men are dying. What does it matter? They're all fighting to get back their past, their lost lives, and in such a great getting back there's bound to be blood." He went into the park and walked over to the furnaces to see whether the captain's body had been completely consumed, and on the way he met the taciturn militia-man, who said to him:

"Where've you been?" Without waiting for an answer he added that Captain Ordóñez had disappeared.

"Some of them say he must have gone over to the enemy. What do you think?"

"I shouldn't think so," said Rómulo evasively. "But I didn't have much to do with him, and you never know what other people's real intentions are."

The militiaman was looking at him with indifferent vagueness.

"What I say is, you can't trust professional soldiers."

Rómulo did not want to say anything concrete.

"And what's the opinion of the others?" he asked.

"There's all sorts. There's even one that says he may have been murdered."

"Who says so?"

"I do."

The militiaman put one hand in his trousers pocket and brought out a pin with a particolored ribbon, precisely the medal the captain used to wear. He exhibited it in the palm of his hand. The ribbon was darkly stained behind.

"That's blood."

Rómulo said:

"Might be."

The militiaman showed him something else: a uniform button.

"See it? It's got a castle engraved on it. The captain was in the Engineers, and this button belongs to his uniform."

"Where did you find it?"

"I picked it up about half an hour ago in the hall, near the stairs." And he added: "What do you think of that?"

Rómulo shrugged. He was in a nervous hurry. He wanted to find out at once whether the cremation had been complete or not, and now by broad daylight and in front of the militiaman it seemed impossible to do so. He told him he could count on him to make investigations and walked away. He went to the tower to tell the duchess about his conversation with the militiaman.

She said:

"That man suspects you. Sooner or later he'll know it was you."

Rómulo felt terribly surprised:

"Me?"

But the duchess asked him what else they were saying about Captain Ordóñez, and he shrugged: "I haven't heard anything more; I only got back just now." All at once, the duchess said nervously:

"You must give me back my pistol."

Rómulo pulled it out and gave it to her. He went over to the radiator and put his hand on it with an inquiring gesture. The duchess seemed to be taking no notice of him, but she turned round like a little animal ready to bite:

"Don't do that again."

Rómulo sat down on the divan with the puppets and picked up one of those lying behind his back. The

puppet's arms ended in little pink hands. On Rómulo's
fist it wagged its head, put its hands to its mouth or its
belly. The latter gesture looked rather like a brazen
allusion—thought Rómulo—but the duchess was smiling. He fetched the bandit, "Candelas," and fitted him
on his other hand. When the duchess saw them approach one another in the air and bow, she smiled
again. Rómulo realized she was fully clad under her
coat. "She doesn't want to risk another scene like that
one," he was thinking.

"You're happy," she said, glancing at him with
rancor.

"Happier than you."

"Yes. It's easy to be happier than me. You can see
I laugh easily, but you know there's no joy in my
laughter."

"What is there, then?"

"Despair and rage."

"Against what?"

"Against the whole world."

How odd for the duchess to talk like that, thought
Rómulo. Later he wanted to put his hand on the radiator but refrained. Since he was unable to do so, he
looked at it instead. He was going to pick up another
puppet when he heard shouts in the park. The duchess
said hastily:

"Rómulo, they're calling you."

She was afraid of somebody coming up to the tower
to look for him. Rómulo, who at that moment was

169

staring absent-mindedly at the carpet, trying to see masculine footprints, rose lazily, went down to the park, walked across it from one side to the other, and, finding nobody about, sat down opposite the ruins of his home and remained gazing at the rows of bricks and stacks of metal arranged in orderly heaps. "I'm not glad of Balbina's death," he was telling himself, "though when she was alive I wasn't glad of her happiness, either." He expected to be called again, but time went by and nobody seemed to think of him. He looked at the havoc the bombardment had wrought in the lawns and gravel of the park. There were three enormous bomb craters. He had spoken to the militiamen about the need of fixing up the place, and they had all answered with evasions except Estradera, who promised to help him. Catching sight of him now, he asked him:

"When are we going to get started on the job?"

Estradera pointed to his bandaged head as a reason for postponing the work. Rómulo clicked his tongue with annoyance. He returned to his room in the basement, regretting the phantom voices that had snatched him from the duchess' presence. As soon as he was alone there, he looked for a small metal tube, found one on the handle of a paint-brush stuck in a perfume bottle, and tried to reproduce the kind of voice he had heard puppet masters use in his childhood. He succeeded easily and spent nearly the whole morning practicing. As he had to say something, he addressed

170

himself in this voice, which sounded rather like the yowling of a cat in heat.

"She's said it. I'm happy! But she's not! Death jumped into the park from her window. And it fell on Balbina, on lots of poor men who wanted to get back their youth the same as you. And you, Rómulo, you forgave her. You haven't only forgiven her, you're willing to hang Balbina's corpse round your neck for the rest of your life, if you confess you're glad of her death. You're not glad of it, Rómulo. That would be the first victory of her ladyship's lover. The first step in your conscience, Rómulo. And, if you get into that, it'll gnaw at your entrails like a worm gnawing inside a fruit."

Rómulo paused. There was an echo in the corner nearest the *salle d'armes*, and the grotesque voice seemed to go out into the corridor and come back again. Rómulo settled the metal tube more firmly in his mouth and continued:

"Everything's changed. Life's taken a turn, and, through blood, death, crime, and war, it's come nearer to you. Anyone would think that as you didn't go after life in your forty lost years, life's come after you, seeking you out in your corner. What's to be done? Life's life, and the duchess seems stronger than ever. She jeers at life and death, but she doesn't jeer at you. Or maybe she does, too, and you don't see it. It's only because she jeers at you that she can ask you to pay

171

for the captain's death with your head, as though you'd been the one to murder him."

He was suddenly startled at hearing himself with the little metal tube in his mouth.

"What am I doing here?"

The first time he asked himself this question, his voice came out still deformed. He removed the small tube, put it in his pocket, and went out. He strolled about the park once more, waiting vainly for the same phantom voice to call him again, and catching sight of the ground-floor windows in the tower—the closed rooms—he asked himself: "Was it Balbina's voice calling me, the way the mother duchess' voice called that time?" He went back to the third floor, and when he saw the duchess she said:

"I haven't slept. Neither have you. Nobody sleeps. Why doesn't anybody get any sleep?"

Rómulo began looking cautiously at the carpet again, seeking the unknown man's footprints. He thought he had found some at the foot of the divan, in the place nearest the bedroom door. Rómulo told the duchess he had several times thought of volunteering for the front. He told her that if he could not do anything for her safety—if she persisted in living up here and receiving visitors—it seemed to him a good solution to go to the front. He was looking at the puppets and heard the duchess say:

"Are you going to leave now, when all these dangers are crowding round me?"

"Exactly. If it's these dangers you want, what can I do about it?"

With astounding naturalness and frivolity, she said:

"Offer your head, as you said you would."

He looked at her, bewildered.

"I'll do it for you. But not for anyone else. I'd rather go to the front and take my chance honorably, the same as others."

He was looking at the puppets. The judge's head was half turned away, and the profile of his bearded cheek gave the impression that he was laughing. Rómulo thought those puppets, so alive and expressive, seemed to be mocking him. He rose, went toward her, and took her by the arm with complete spontaneity.

"That man you want me to give my life for. Who is he?"

"Rómulo, let go of me. I don't want you to give your life for anybody."

"Answer me. Who is that man?"

"Rómulo, don't ask me to be an informer."

"I want you to tell me who he is and why you want to force me to die like a rat for a crime I haven't committed."

The chorus of puppets seemed to be laughing. The duchess managed to release herself and was smiling too. Rómulo went into the bedroom again. He found nobody. He came out, went to the stairs, mounted to the fourth and fifth floors, and made sure there was no one there either. He was saying to himself: "She

173

and he are on a level where you can ask a man who's innocent to die a vile death. I don't want to get onto that level." But even if he had wanted to get onto it, he realized he could not easily have reached it. When he returned to the duchess' room, he saw the puppets and felt rebuffed. The duchess said it was cold and three of the radiators were not working. She knew that by giving him routine orders she would manage to deflect him from his excitement, and she told him she would go down to the second floor of the tower if the radiators there were hot. She begged him to go and make sure about it. Rómulo went down to the second floor. The hangings there were pale violet. In the place of the Zurbarán was a copy of El Greco's "Resurrection," which looked as though it had been painted with blood, white lead, and oxide of copper. In the back room he glimpsed the top of a marble staircase leading down to the floor below, to the rooms where the duchess' mother had died. When Rómulo returned he drew her attention to this, and she shrugged wearily.

They started down. Rómulo made several trips back to bring her the things she asked for, and on the last one he fetched the Punch-and-Judy puppets. He stumbled over the captain's shoe. "The duchess must have stumbled over it, too," he told himself. In his arms the puppets seemed living, animate creatures that might escape. Living, but more like chickens or rabbits than people.

174

When he was at last ready to leave, having put cushions in all the windows, to deaden the sound of voices as well as to prevent the lights from showing at night or the cold air from getting in, he heard the duchess say:

"Rómulo, please don't speak to me again the way you did today."

There was a tone of entreaty in her voice that touched Rómulo. "She loves that man," he thought, "in spite of herself. Who knows if she isn't getting back a part of her lost youth, also, by going to him?" But he did not want to accept it. He could not accept it, and that was all. He bent his head and went out.

From the duchess' diary:

"Two more days and nights of orgies with the 'devil.'

"Rómulo seems ready for anything. That's why I must get ready, too, and leave here at once to take my chance of salvation or destruction.

"I have to get some adequate clothes. And papers."

It was a gloomy morning. The sun seemed to have gone forever. At ten o'clock it was still as dark as it had been at dawn. Rómulo asked López to help him clear up the damage the bombs had done to the lawn, but every time he spoke of the matter they all tried to wriggle out of it. "They're scared of shovels and pick-axes," he thought, "as though they were going to bite them." He went over to the furnaces and found the body completely consumed. The ashes had retained the shape of the captain's body, and Rómulo wanted to break them up with an iron hook but could not nerve himself to it. Coming back, he met the taciturn militiaman looking for him. He had been to the district municipal laboratory and had just returned. He showed him the captain's pin again.

"They've analyzed this stain, and it's blood."

"That's what I said," Rómulo told him, mastering his agitation, and after a pause he added: "What do you think can have happened?"

The militiaman looked him in the face.

"Sooner or later we'll know."

He was turning the pin over and over between his fingers. Suddenly he asked:

"Where are you living now?"

"In the basement."

The militiaman ran a vague glance over the ground floor of the palace.

"Have you got a fireplace for burning wood?"

"No."

"How do you heat your coffee?"

"I've got a little electric stove."

That hint—thought Rómulo—showed the militiaman was on the right track. "They're going to kill me like a coward, like a traitor, a wretch, and I'll have to die for that other man." The soldiers, evidently about to set out for the front, were working at one end of the park. Rómulo asked:

176

"Have those boys been given their kits for leaving yet?"

"Yes. They're going tonight."

The militiaman added:

"The relieving's always done at night."

But he returned to the theme:

"Some day you're going to show me where you live."

"Do you want to come over now?"

The militiaman gazed at him with a faraway look and shook his head. When Rómulo parted from the militiaman at the garage door, he returned to the palace more worried than ever. He knew Cartridge would go on investigating, and in that case he was bound to discover everything somehow or other. He was going about his investigations slowly but surely. He was not only suspicious, he had even formed a plan in which Rómulo was somehow involved. Rómulo walked over to the soldiers who were getting ready to leave, and a corporal asked him:

"Well, Rómulo, aren't you coming?"

"You're saying it in fun," answered Rómulo, "but others might do worse than me. I was a corporal in Morocco."

He noticed that the taciturn militiaman seemed to be listening. Aware of that watchfulness, he asked:

"When are you leaving?"

"At dusk."

Rómulo hesitated, but ended by saying:

"Before you go, I'll come and give you my final answer."

This was almost a promise, and some of the soldiers received it with cheers, although—Rómulo was telling himself—their cheers were merely the continuance of the joke. Shortly afterward, Rómulo went to the duchess and said without much conviction:

"I'm leaving tonight with the boys· of the antitank company."

The duchess seemed surprised.

"It's a useless piece of rashness."

Rómulo, turning pale, said:

"If I don't get killed, I think I can get back on leave in a couple of weeks' time."

He now seemed pleased, and the duchess observed his lightheartedness narrowly without comprehending it. Nevertheless, she said·:

"It's stupid to go off like that."

Rómulo offered to stay on condition she would let him block up the stairs that very night. She shook her head slowly. Rómulo got ready to go and said, referring to the duchess and her lover:

"Then take care."

The duchess glanced away.

"Any amount of care will be useless, I suppose."

Rómulo tried to give her some advice on practical details—food, heating—but she interrupted him:

"That's all right. Now go."

Rómulo looked long and silently at her, and with

178

a great effort he walked out. He headed for the *salle d'armes*, fetched a leather hunting jacket, and then went out to the park by a service door and to the furnaces, where with a long hook he broke up the human figure whose outline was still preserved by the ashes. That gave him. a sensation of repugnance. Then he went back to where the soldiers were and demanded a dynamiter's outfit. When he had the straps on, and the regulation load of hand grenades, and the pistol at his side, the taciturn militiaman approached him and looked slowly at him without saying anything. They were starting off. At the gate, Ruiz, who was on sentry duty, said as he saw him pass:

"That's the way for a man to act, Rómulo."

These words accompanied him nearly as far as the Toledo Bridge, where they were driven from his mind. But, exactly the same as last time, as soon·as he left the house he seemed to be nearer to the duchess than ever, more keenly aware of all his problems. "Perhaps," he told himself with distaste, "one of these days the police'll come and take me away from the front, to have me shot behind the lines. And what'll I say? What'll I do?" Somewhat further along the Manzanares, a few mortar shells fell. As he saw them burst, Lieutenant Uriarte came out of his boredom to say:

"What a way to receive us! With little mortars."

He seemed comically disappointed and added:

"Last time, they at least received us with shells from the six-inch guns."

CHAPTER
FIVE

THE DUCHESS WAITED FOR THE "DEVIL," BUT HE did not appear for three nights. Her loneliness at night, and her sensation, during the day, of being helpless without Rómulo, bewildered her. A swarm of new feelings descended on her and at times tortured her. The presence of the Punch-and-Judy puppets, instead of giving her an inner tranquillity as it had on the day she found them, only moved her to tenderness, and this tenderness—which was the fond memory of her own childhood—weakened her. In the absence of Estéban's cynical laughter, any sentimental allusion to her present or her past left her feeling even more lonely and defenseless.

"Estéban hasn't come. Is he afraid? If he's afraid, then all his cynicism was a piece of poor play-acting. Or is it that cynicism springs from fear and is nothing but a sorry defense?" The "devil" had killed the captain and forty-eight other men, and Balbina. Now the "devil" had realized that suspicions were beginning to veer toward him and meant a growing danger; but since when had the "devil" eschewed danger? How could he possibly give her up through fear and leave all the danger to her, to the duchess? Several times she had thought of the possibility of going to live in Estéban's "stamping ground." This expression— stamping ground of the devil—fascinated her.

She reflected that Estéban had not told her anything concrete about his clandestine life in Madrid. Not where he lived. Nor what he did. The duchess realized that Estéban might have used precautions and stratagems with her. Perhaps, considering the prudence of such reserves insufficient, he had stopped visiting the tower so as not to run too many risks. And he had cut off his visits without telling her about it, taking care she should not guess his intentions or his alarm. She had spoken to him about the riskiness of the new situation, and he had laughed at it, feigning confidence, but at the same time he might have been deciding not to return to the palace any more. And he decided it without telling her. Deceiving her. He had not even told her where the famous stamping ground was. To the duchess, this seemed too vile to be true, but the mere fact of having thought it broke up a great many things within her. "I need," she said to herself, "to keep my faith in somebody."

After the first two days of her solitude, she was left without provisions. "One night I'll go down to the cellar," she said to herself. She had no books, either. She had read the ones in the tower several times, all except the volume by the Marquis de Sade. "We women know too much about love to be interested in that sort of problem. Men get all puffed up with pride, thinking they're discovering the secrets of love at every step. But any sixteen-year-old virgin has them all vividly in her blood."

During the long hours of boredom, she turned back to *Examples of Monarchies*. She could read it only at night, when she thought the other inhabitants of the palace were asleep. By day, she wandered listlessly about, full of anguish as to what might be happening around her. At night, however, she managed to take her mind off it, and amidst all the difficulties and dangers—under the constant faraway throb of battle—she could even feel happy in being able to set herself moral problems beyond the bounds of her reality. The cold in the tower was dry and persistent and, not finding enough reaction in her blood, it pierced her to the bone. The book of *Examples* began with a poetic project for studying historically the most famous monarchies of the past. This poetic project consisted in the following: "The universe is an immense monarchy. We, as dwellers in the universe, must fatally submit to it, and, in our turn, are kings of that reality which makes up our existence. Everything which man has dreamed, dared, created, has been done because of this monarchy of man—king—and his illusion—queen. Man—the king—and his ideal ambition—the queen." The book went into curious considerations. It said that the relationship between the king and the queen, in this glorious and fertile marriage, ought to be like any relationship between a man and a woman, within the limits which God has imposed on the possession of one human being by another. And the duchess reread these lines with pleasure, satisfied at being able to linger calmly over such problems: "But when the king—man—desireth to fulfill himself in the ideal possession of the queen, even unto attaining the absolute of God, then is the harmony destroyed and the order of matrimony ended. For to attain ambition is to slay the same, and to realize therein the ambition of self-ideal is beyond the power of man, save by passing through death and misfortune." To the duchess, this seemed poetically true. And she was grateful to herself for still being capable of making such "de luxe" reflections.

One night, after rereading these lines, she said to herself as she listened to the battle din as usual: "From the fifth-floor terrace, the whole east side of Madrid ought to be visible." She had never before thought that war might be a show. She went up to the terrace. It was a very dark night. She could not easily have been seen. The night cold—the open air—was of a different kind from the cold in her rooms. Out in that huge night, where the horizons, the darkness, and the high vault of the sky seemed animate and alive, the cold became an ulterior, irrelevant circumstance. When she thought about it, it eventually turned into a species of voluptuousness. Far away, spreading from north to south over an area of about fifteen or twenty miles, the horizon looked like an irregular, continuous series of red stars of different sizes that kept lighting up or flickering out ceaselessly. When the wind was in the right direction, rifle and machine-gun shots could be heard quite plainly. Between them—they sounded dry and mechanical—would come the rougher, deeper noise of a hand grenade or more luminous explosions from a mortar. Meanwhile, from time to time shells would pass in droves over the duchess' head, and she thought: "It's cold, but I don't feel it; or, rather, I feel it as a moral circumstance. On the other hand, I can feel terror; it's like a physical fact." And she stayed on there. Looking at the horizon and watching that chain of stars, sometimes interrupted here and there and often wider in one place than in another, she repeated to herself: "Rómulo's out there. Perhaps he lit one of those red stars." And she thought of Rómulo with gratitude. Not the gratitude of a person who feels protected, but another kind of gratitude that she could not for the moment define. "I'm his ideal ambition, his illusion." The duchess had known this for a long time, but until after the night of the bombardment it had seemed to her merely a pic-

184

turesque fact, something almost grotesque. Since that night, everything had been different, and her gratitude toward this man who "dreamed her" was a rather unreal and idle sentiment. That was why she enjoyed it. This reflection alarmed her.

"I'm still outside of life, beyond the borders of reality, playing with it, perhaps, and with myself. Playing. Playing, as usual. If life summons me once again to the truth of men and things, in what horrible way will the summons come?"

She recalled the first summons—the duke's death—and the second—the "devil," the reflector, the corpses in the park, the captain bleeding to death on the carpet. But once the first moment of surprise had passed, something within her rose above all these realities, and she not only regained her poise, but laughed aloud, perhaps wanting to incorporate that merriment in "God's huge roar of laughter." At that very moment, on the terrace, while she watched death riding by on clouds of fire, in convoys of iron, or saw him sending his exact messages in the little red stars, she was setting herself "de luxe" problems—man and his illusion, the king and the queen—which, when all was said and done, was merely a way of laughing, a haughty way of laughing.

Planes were flying over the front lines. They dropped their bombs in bunches on a not very extensive area. And before the explosions reached the duchess' ears clouds of green, yellow, reddish smoke,

185

violently combined, rose in silence. Then the air around the duchess shook and revealed its false depths in the profound vibrations of the reports. Something flamed up beneath those clouds, and the colors—yellow, green, reddish—persisted. The duchess saw that it was like a gigantic projection on the black of the night of the "Resurrection" of El Greco, which she had in her apartment. Jesus, nude, with his twisted thighs, and an ascending impulsion of sudden flame rose in the air. The presence of that gigantic Son of God impressed the duchess, who nevertheless reacted with sarcasm:

"Sometimes I'd like to say to God: 'Yes; good, evil, life, death, You and Your eternity. That's all very well, but what of it?' "

The duchess knew she was stronger out there on the terrace. "When I return to the bedroom, the worries will come back." And she delayed returning, thinking about Rómulo as a familiar being to whose presence she had grown accustomed. She did not condemn him for having gone away, for having left his post in the house. It was an offense coupled with a tribute. "Maybe he's gone out there to be more alone with me." And later on she thought: "Estéban hasn't come back to my room for fear of danger. Yet Rómulo's gone away for fear of a kind of debasement—'offering his head for Estéban'—and he's gone to look for danger, to give his life somewhere else, under honorable conditions."

186

The duchess remained on the terrace for a long while. The wind, the cold, and that fierce and sublime spectacle enfolded her in a voluptuous panic which she had already known. Finally she returned to her bedroom. Perhaps she would find Estéban there. But he had not come. Catching sight of the Renaissance cover of *Examples of Monarchies*, with its wood-engravings of angels and columns and plinths, she thought of Rómulo again. "Rómulo the King. I the Queen." This "de luxe" reflection struck her as amusing.

But she was hungry, and she began to calculate the risks of an expedition to the cellar. At last, with a pocket flashlight as small and slim as a pencil, and the mother-of-pearl pistol, both held in the same hand, she went down. She was a long time reaching the cellar. She entered it without turning on the lights or making any sound. In one corner she heard an alarming noise, like the snores of somebody asleep. She was about to take flight, but the beam of her flashlight accidentally fell on Midge, who was sleeping in a corner huddled among his rags. She went over to him. The midget appeared even smaller and looked like a sprite or a gnome. The duchess' first impression was that she had suddenly come upon one of those magic beings she had believed in as a child. But the dwarf's ugliness frightened her more than any known danger. She was going to run away at the very moment when the midget woke up and sprang to his feet. Knowing

187

he had been discovered, he picked up a big stick near him and, grasping it with both hands, prepared to defend himself. Just then the duchess' fingers slipped involuntarily from the button on her flashlight, and the light went out. In the darkness she heard the voice of the midget, who was not quite awake:

"Don't move another step!"

The duchess pressed the light on again. The midget jerked up his arm to cover his face with it, as though the light had struck him, and growled:

"Look out! Don't move another step, or I'll hit you with this club."

The duchess asked:

"Who are you? What are you doing here?"

Dazzled by the flashlight, the midget could not see the duchess. He calmed down on hearing her voice.

"Excuse me. I'm Alexander the wax-chandler."

"What are you doing here?"

"I'm waiting for victory. Rómulo knows I'm here, and he lets me stay and doesn't say anything. Though he took my weapons away from me the first day, I do what I can. I'm guarding Their Graces' food."

He spat on his hands and brandished the club again, but not in a threatening manner. The duchess went on looking at him without being able to understand. Though the midget could not see her, he was looking in her direction, and she had a feeling the look soiled her. Suddenly the midget took a bound up the wall and reached the switch, and the lights came on. Seeing the duchess, the dwarf dropped the stick, covered himself up as well as he could, for he was almost naked, and stepped forward.

"Is it Her Grace, the duchess?"

She did not reply, and finally she also asked:

"You said just now you were guarding the food. Against whom are you guarding it?"

The dwarf pointed to the passageway and was hesitant about answering.

"It isn't a matter for Her Grace's ears," he said at length.

But the duchess stood there waiting, full of interrogations and perplexities, and the midget spoke.

"It's Chrissie. Chrissie's the worst of them. I work in a wax-chandlery. There's always a rat in wax-chandleries that eats the Christmas candles."

The duchess listened to him, thinking:

"This—man, sprite, gnome—is ugly and oughtn't to be alive, but he is alive."

The midget went on:

"I call that kind of rat Chrissie. There aren't any candles here. But there's a Chrissie."

After a long pause, he added:

"She's the worst. The male's not very smart, but Chrissie knows too much and jumps right at me, because she knows the club's no good in hand-to-hand fighting."

The duchess noticed that the midget's arms were

covered with scratches. She was going to ask him something, but he continued:

"Chrissie's got her strength in her hindquarters and her shoulders. She jumps like a monkey. I haven't been able to get at her with the club, and so far her teeth and nails are stronger than mine."

The duchess retreated. From the threshold, she asked with staring eyes:

"But do you fight?"

"Yes."

"With the rats?"

"So far, only with Chrissie."

The duchess drew back, speechless, and got as far as the storeroom. The door was locked with the key in it. She entered, picked up some things, and came rushing out as though she had stolen them. The midget went along down the passage behind her.

"Doesn't Her Grace want any wine?"

The duchess would not have stopped to look at him again for anything in the world. The midget was still following her and saying:

"Will you let me go on living here? Will you really let me go on keeping watch and guarding the provisions? Just till our people enter Madrid."

She went up to her rooms in the darkness, repeating, startled: "Our people. He said 'our people.'" When she arrived, she dropped down on the bed and was unable to sleep all night, thinking about the midget and seeing him bite the rat as he struggled with it.

190

The following day she could not eat either and kept repeating to herself:

"I must get out of here."

When she thought of leaving the palace her imagination took her to Estéban's "stamping ground." But where could that place be?

The house seemed hateful to her, and she would wake up during the night with sudden starts of terror. She could not understand how Rómulo could have omitted to speak to her about this individual. "It's really the last straw—something I never would have been able to imagine." She spent whole hours mulling over it, and at night she would keep looking around her, without seeing anything, trying to identify doubtful noises. If a piece of furniture creaked, she would think it might be Chrissie or Gimlet with some of the dwarf's blood on her or his whiskers.

And Estéban did not come back. The duchess condemned him at times, but all her reproaches exploded before the idea that he might have been killed. She thought that when her provisions were used up she would rather die of hunger than see the midget again. After the encounter, she remembered her words on the terrace that night: "Good, evil, life, death, eternity. That's all very well, but what of it?" She remembered them, and they seemed like a horrible blasphemy to her. And a voice, her own voice, but projected inward, repeated: "I must get out of here."

One afternoon, she heard voices in the park below

her window. The militiamen had seen that one of the outside wooden shutters had almost been wrenched off by the explosions on the night of the bombardment and was hanging uncertainly from its last hinges. The militiamen wanted to pull it down, because there was a danger the wind might unhitch it and drop it on somebody. They came with a long rope and threw it up to the window over and over again, until it caught on the wood. The first few times they threw it up, the rope smacked against the broken panes and some bits of glass even fell into the room. This made the duchess think she had been discovered and that the militiamen —one of whom was talking about going up to pull the shutter off from the inside—were already in the tower. The others said it was so shaky it would come down at the first tug of the rope. But the duchess did not know whether the militiaman who had spoken first was on his way up or not, and she stood waiting near the stairs with the little pistol in her hand. When she heard the militiamen, who had managed to lasso the window, pulling on the rope, and finally succeeding in tearing off the shutter, and then receiving its fall into the park with shouts of childish glee, she breathed more easily and said to herself: "I'm so used to danger that when a threat isn't fulfilled, it's like a disappointment."

A soldier was skipping the rope and humorously singing the song that little girls are sometimes heard singing in the parks:

"Merceditas already is dead
She is dead for I have seen her. . . ."
The duchess finished it in her imagination:

"There were four dukes who carried her
Through the streets of Madrid."

The song referred to the young Queen Mercedes, who had died in the last third of the past century. "My father," she said to herself, "was one of those four dukes and could not hear that song without tears coming to his eyes." Recalling the circumstances of the death of her own mother, the duchess murmured: "How could a sentimental man like my father give rise to that gossip?"

The following night she went up to the terrace again, but, when she came out on it, she saw the moon was shining and drew back frightened. She returned to her rooms, but the shutter incident had made the place uncomfortable and suspect, and she thought of going down to the floor below. But this was already the floor with the rooms where her mother had died, and she could not nerve herself to it. Besides, the windows in that room were too low down, within anybody's reach. She considered going to the basement room—near the pool—but if the "devil" arrived he would not find her, and she dreaded the idea of being so near the midget's cellar and the gigantic rats.

She thought about Rómulo's return with impatience. "But maybe I've already asked too much of him, and he'll never come back." These ideas wearied her, and again she told herself: "I must get out of here; I must escape." She went down cautiously at night to fetch Balbina's clothes, meaning to disguise herself in them. She left them on the bed, spread out at the foot. They were there for several days. She used to look at them sometimes, undecided. One night she put them on. When she saw the "Resurrection" of El Greco she thought of the projection enlarged upon the black background of the night, which she had seen from the terrace. And she imagined Rómulo buried in that darkness.

Rómulo had been wounded and sent to the hospital. A mortar shell had sprayed one of his legs with shrapnel. But three days later he was able to get up and hop about the hospital on crutches. As his wounds were not serious and required no special treatment, he asked to be allowed to go home. They drove him over in a car, and he stepped down into the palace park with a bandaged leg and two sticks. Every morning he had to go to the nearest first-aid station to have the wounds dressed. The first day he was accompanied by Cartridge, whose suspicions seemed to have vanished. As the taciturn militiaman was no longer thinking about Rómulo in connection with the disappearance of Captain Ordóñez, the palace atmosphere was one of quiet trust.

Some militiamen returning from the Carabanchel front, who had not been in the palace before, started to talk about the events of the last few days and often referred to "Rómulo's Rock." Rómulo asked them why they called it that, and they told him wonderful tales about the heroism of an individual bearing his name who had defended the rock under incredible circumstances. The number of tanks destroyed by this hero kept getting higher and higher, and soon they were talking about fourteen. It appeared that even the General Staff called the place "Rómulo's Rock" when they mentioned it. Rómulo said with a mixture of manly diffidence and pride:

"I am that Rómulo."

When the militiamen learned of it, they changed their attitude toward Rómulo. They regarded him as a superior being. Without his having asked it of them, López and Estradera began clearing up the bomb wreckage in the park.

Rómulo found the duchess very pale. On seeing his bandaged leg, she questioned him with her glance. Having him there in front of her made him once again a servant, and the duchess felt his absence as a meaningless parenthesis. Rómulo told her his wound was of no consequence.

"We've all been lucky, if you can call it luck to be still alive."

She immediately forgot about it and began reproaching him. The tower was uninhabitable. She had had to keep on drinking the remaining wine so as not to die of cold. Then she told him about the horrible encounter in the cellar. Rómulo gave a half-smile.

"So you've seen him?"

"How could you let him get in?" she asked, annoyed.

Rómulo made no reply. Looking at the puppets on the divan, he asked them mentally: "How are you, my friends? Are you having a good time with the duchess?" She persisted in talking about the midget, and Rómulo persisted in smiling without answering. He winced with pain as he moved his leg. She inquired how he had been wounded; he told her the facts and afterward added jokingly what they were ascribing to him. He lingered, rather gratified, over the account of "Rómulo's Rock." There was a kind of primitive and authentic glory in it. The picture by El Greco continued to be war, all war. And in it Rómulo was producing fires and explosions. She said, smiling:

"A hero."

"Pooh, they put you in a difficult place, and you do the best you can in it. Afterward, other people like to talk, that's all."

She glanced at Rómulo with an indifference already familiar to him.

"My people don't aim very well."

"Are you saying that because they didn't kill me?"

"And because they didn't kill everybody, the night of the bombardment."

Rómulo thought there was something false in her voice. He got up and went toward her and, in doing so without his sticks, fell down on his good knee with his other leg stretched out and saw the duchess trying, unsuccessfully, not to laugh. Rómulo had known that laugh quite well ever since the already faraway day in the swimming pool. He got up with difficulty. His awkwardness made the duchess laugh still more. He looked for one of the sticks, and, when at last he was leaning on it, he asked:

"Why are you laughing?"

The duchess challenged him with her indifference:

"What do you want me to do—cry?"

Sitting down on the divan, Rómulo said:

"Aren't you ashamed of laughing at a cripple? Laughing at someone else's misfortune is a useless cruelty."

"There's nothing useless, Rómulo, in real cruelty."

Rómulo thought the clandestine lover still visited her every night. There was something willfully hard, cynical, and violent about her. Rómulo thought as he stared at her: "If the duchess were really as she thinks she is, I wouldn't do what I'm doing for her." He wanted to make a test. He reached behind him on the divan and suddenly found Uncle Babu in one hand and Aunt Misery in the other. The duchess in her coat was shivering with cold. Rómulo told her he would light the furnaces during the night, although there was very little coal left. He put down the puppets he had picked up and took hold of the peasant woman and the farrier. He sat looking attentively at the peasant woman and said: "She's like Balbina." Then he placed the little metal tube he had taken from his pocket in his mouth and, distorting his voice grotesquely, began:

BALBINA

"Ring-around the roses, a pocketful of posies, old blood, new blood, we all fall down. Oh, dear, oh, dear, oh, dear! Her poor Grace, and I can't sit down at the table until I know she's got all she needs." (*The puppet was rubbing her face with her wooden hands as though drying her tears. Rómulo exaggerated Balbina's crying with grotesque wails. The duchess shifted in her armchair.*) "Oooh, dear, oooh, dear, oooh, dear, the shock's stuck in Her Grace's heart and that's why she can't weep. Poor lady, so young and without His Grace's comforting warmth!"

ENSIGN VINEGAR

"And why does Her Grace have to weep? Why do you want her to weep if she won't weep?"

The duchess looked without comprehending. Rómulo continued imitating a feminine voice.

BALBINA

"May I be torn to shreds, may the dogs eat me, if Her poor Grace can't get some tears of consolation!"

198

CAPTAIN SPARKS

"Why does she have to weep? I'm not a captain. I've been promoted to major. They promoted me for nosing about the stairs."

The duchess blinked nervously. Rómulo went on, impassible.

BALBINA

"I thought it was the other way round; I thought they'd taken you down a peg."

CAPTAIN SPARKS

"That was later, in the elevator. It wasn't Her Grace. Nor the master, either."

BALBINA

"And didn't they give you a medal?"

CAPTAIN SPARKS

"Yes. They gave me a cross. A cross with a pension. The Grand Cross of the Split Skull Convention."

The duchess was staring at Rómulo, acutely pale. She seemed to want to say something and to be holding it back with difficulty. Rómulo picked up two other dolls and went on, with a half smile in the left corner of his mouth:

199

AUNT MISERY

"Oooh, dear, oh, dear, oh, dear! How frightful, how tragically shocking! And now I've got nothing left to put in my stocking!"

UNCLE BABU

"You haven't anything left to put in your stocking? Why worry? Here I am, legless, hatless, nameless. My right leg landed in Ventas del Espiritu Santo and my left in Recoletas."

AUNT MISERY

"What's the captain up to? I haven't seen him around lately."

UNCLE BABU

"He's been heating the duchess' bath water for the last week."

The duchess straightened up and seemed to want to talk. She made a rigid movement of her torso, from left to right. "She seems like a marionette, too," Rómulo thought and continued:

AUNT MISERY

"Were there a lot of men at Rómulo's house that night?"

UNCLE BABU

"Forty-eight. They were all left legless, like

Balbina, with their guts torn open and smoke coming out of their bread-baskets."

AUNT MISERY

"I saw a silver light on a rat's nose in the night."

UNCLE BABU

"I saw a gold one full on the horns of a bull."

AUNT MISERY

"They say it was flares."

UNCLE BABU

"The captain thought otherwise and went to see if his belief was right and died like a martyr for his faith."

The duchess' pallor was greater, and her hand was trembling on the chair arm. She spoke: "Rómulo, this is cruel. It is too much, Rómulo. Please. . . ." Rómulo thought: "She talks like a marionette," and with his eyes on hers he went on with his farce:

AUNT MISERY

"How did it happen, Uncle Babu?"

UNCLE BABU

"He stuck his head into the tower and 'bang!

201

bang!' Two shots. One in the wall and the other in his forehead."

AUNT MISERY

"Who gave him half a pair like that?"

UNCLE BABU

"Some say she did, and some say he as well. Rómulo knows but he won't tell."

AUNT MISERY

"You won't tell, either, except in code."

UNCLE BABU

"I can't say anything more."

AUNT MISERY

"Did they knock him cold at one go?"

UNCLE BABU

"No. And it was his own fault."

AUNT MISERY

"Why?"

UNCLE BABU

"For getting his head in the bullet's way. And then for scratching the wound. That was when the blood . . . slid down his face."

The duchess stood up. Her face was ashen. She tried to get to the bedroom but before reaching the door she fell full length on the carpet. Her eyes were open, and an expression of terror seemed to linger in them. Rómulo hurried over to her. He went to the bathroom and returned with the same damp towel he had once wanted to use on Captain Ordóñez. He applied the towel to her temples. He had to move about slowly, leaning on his stick, staggering.

The duchess showed no signs of coming to. Rómulo laid his hands on her face, and it felt cold. He went back to the bathroom and, finding a small bottle of brandy, poured a few drops between her lips. The duchess did not revive. Rómulo put a cushion under her head, stepped back, and sat down on the divan. A little later he decided to carry her over to the bed. It was not easy to pick her up in his arms. In order to lay her down, Rómulo had to take some of Balbina's clothes off the bed where they were spread out: a skirt, a blouse, a coat, a head kerchief, even a pair of run-down shoes. Rómulo tossed them all on the floor. When he saw the duchess lying in bed, covered to the waist, he felt better, but she still showed no signs of life. Rómulo kissed her on the mouth. Ashamed, he drew back a little and waited. He kissed her again, gently this time, and had gone back to staring at Balbina's clothes on the floor when he heard the duchess speak. She muttered something confusedly, weeping. Rómulo saw how graceful, delicate, and almost humble she looked, and he let her weep, thinking: "It's good for her to cry." He asked her:

"How are you feeling?"

"All right, quite all right."

Rómulo took one of her hands, which felt freezing, in both of his.

"Take it easy, now." He glanced at his wife's clothes again. "Did you go and get them from the basement room?"

"Yes."

"You've been thinking of going away?"

"Yes."

"Where to?"

"I don't know."

The duchess was thinking of Estéban's "stamping ground." Then of Valencia. Of going alone to Valencia. Rómulo tried to dissuade her:

"Perhaps living here won't be so dangerous now."

"Why?"

"Seeing me like this, with my leg bandaged, nobody'll suspect me."

The tower was cold. Rómulo said he was going to light the furnaces. The duchess kept staring at his soldier's belt, with the pistol—worn openly now—on one side of it and a dagger on the other. Rómulo went off, telling himself: "There isn't any level where she and he can urge death on me and laugh about it. Maybe there is for him, but not for her."

As he was walking down the central avenue of the park, thinking it would be impossible to approach the furnaces without being seen, the taciturn militiaman came to meet him:

"What do you think of this?" he said, displaying the buckle of a burnt belt in his hand, with its metal half melted.

He also showed him a pistol magazine warped by fire. To Rómulo's amazement he kept adding more articles, among them something as unmistakable as the captain's identity bracelet, with his number. Rómulo was growing jumpy, but the militiaman was far from suspecting him.

"Tomorrow," he said suddenly, "we'll know all about it. We'll know who killed him, who set those furnaces going and burned him up. Early tomorrow morning."

Rómulo tried to feel his bandaged foot touching the ground, and the contact gave him a reassurance which lasted for a few moments.

"How's that?"

The militiaman told him a woman had walked up to him while he was on sentry duty two days earlier and said she knew who had killed the officer. "Don't you think that's odd?" Rómulo tried to give free range to his nerves by glancing about at the grass, the trees, the gray sky. The militiaman went on: "I've got her name here." He took out a slip of paper and read:

205

"Joaquina Pérez, widow of Antonio Pérez, plumber. Obtain a passport for evacuation to Valencia." The militiaman added:

"Women can leave Madrid whenever they like, and dead militiamen's relations are given priority, so it's not hard to get a passport. But all this fuss about it has made me suspicious."

"Is the passport just for her, or for more people as well?"

"No, just for her."

"What did she say?"

"This is exactly what she said: 'I know everything, but I won't say a word until I'm sure of leaving Madrid.' I asked her for some proof that she was telling the truth, and she said: 'Look among the ashes in the furnaces at the end of the park, and maybe you'll find something.'"

The militiaman displayed the articles again and added:

"These are much more than we'll need."

Rómulo blinked nervously. He would never have believed it. It did not agree with the duchess' behavior of only a short while before, when she had fainted under the puppets' accusations. The militiaman added:

"I thought those furnaces were always out."

"So did I," said Rómulo.

"The whole point is to find out who lit them."

Rómulo could not understand how he was still able

to go on talking, but he did so, imagining the duchess dressed in Balbina's clothes:

"What have you fixed up?"

"There's a convoy leaving for Valencia very early tomorrow morning, and she's going to come here at daybreak, and I'll give her her papers. In return, she's going to tell me the criminal's name and where we can find him."

Trying to hide his consternation, Rómulo asked him for the articles two or three times and looked at them one by one. Afterward he gave them back.

"Good. In any case, tomorrow we'll know how we stand."

He went away on his sticks in a state of complete dejection. "Shall I have to pay? Shall I have to pay for her lover? How dare they expect it? I've never confessed I'm glad of Balbina's death. I haven't gone over to their camp. How dare they, if I haven't gone over to their camp?" And he went back to thinking that the level where she and her lover waited calmly and smilingly for his death was inaccessible and incomprehensible to him, but nonetheless real.

He counted the hours that were left until the following dawn. He felt lonely. He realized that what he had previously taken for solitude was merely a pleasant connection with everybody, and that true solitude, deep and bitter, was beginning now. Why did the duchess want to make him pay? Night was falling. He watched it coming through the broken window panes.

Although there had been no sunshine during the day, some little pink clouds appeared now, slightly luminous, in the distance, the color of a woman's flesh.

Realizing he had lost everything, he sank into the very depths of despair and—oddly enough—found there a certain appeasement. When it was quite dark he mounted the stairs one by one and went to the tower. He thought he would behave just as usual and wait to see how things turned out. If necessary, he could feign quite as well as she could; better, in fact.

Not finding her in the parlor, he went through to the bedroom. Balbina's clothes were there on a chair beside her.

"When are you going away?"

"Who, I?" she asked, surprised.

"When?" persisted Rómulo. "Tomorrow? Why don't you go tomorrow?"

"No. I can't tomorrow. I won't be able to go for at least a week."

"I'll help you."

"That's not true, Rómulo. Yes, I know you'd give your life to save me, but you wouldn't do anything to send me away from you."

Rómulo was looking at her, and she returned the look tranquilly. A wave of blood seemed to rise toward Rómulo's face and stick in his throat, but the duchess went on speaking: "Yes, Rómulo, I know you'd give your life for me, you'd give it quite willingly, maybe thinking about your friends in other planets. Wouldn't you?" Rómulo thought to himself: "She wants to make sure she'll only be giving me a pleasure by accusing me and sending me to my death. She's up on that high inaccessible level that I'm beginning to understand by this time. I'll answer her from the same place myself."

"It's all going to be different, Rómulo," she said, "from tomorrow on. I know you're my only friend and that you're right. Do you hear? I know you're right. From tomorrow on, it's all going to be different."

Rómulo told himself: "She's saying this now, a few hours before going off and leaving me in the executioner's hands." With a difficult smile he asked:

"From tomorrow on?"

He felt he was on "that level" already. It was not so very hard. It was only a matter of stifling your blood and speaking with a cool, keen mind, inured to cruelty and lies. He felt sure she was not ill. She could lie about her illness, too, like all the rest. The swoon had also been a pretense. He thought he had felt those radiations an animate body gives back when kissed. Rómulo gripped one of her hands.

"From tomorrow on?"

"Yes, Rómulo. But let go of me. You're hurting me."

"Very well, just as you like. From tomorrow on. I'll give you the last thing I can give you."

He was smiling just as he had seen her smile these last few days. But she asked:

"To me?"

209

"Yes. I'll give you the one and only and ultimate thing."

Seeing yet another kind of harmony in the duchess, a harmony full of perfidy, a strength that—somewhere up on that high level—was inaccessible to him, he stood admiring her. She said nothing. Rómulo saw a certain sarcasm behind her silence. She asked:

"Have you spoken to that taciturn militiaman?"

"No," he lied.

"Then he hasn't said anything more to you?"

Rómulo clenched his fist on the sheet.

"No, nothing."

Then, a moment later:

"Don't worry. You shall go. You shall go whenever you like."

He felt satisfied with himself. She answered, realizing perhaps—thought Rómulo—that he knew and accepted everything:

"Yes, Rómulo. Thank you, Rómulo."

For a moment he wavered, thinking he might be mistaken, and decided to put her to the test. He said he was going to take Balbina's clothes away. If she was not thinking of leaving tomorrow, she would not need them. But she objected with sudden energy. Forgetting everything then, Rómulo leaned over the pillow and kissed the duchess on the mouth. She pushed him back. "What are you doing, Rómulo?" He found her mouth again and bit into it until he felt blood on his lips. Then he let go of her. She began to moan dully. A small wound on her upper lip was staining the pillow with blood.

"Beast!"

As she pronounced the "b" she spattered Rómulo's face with blood. Rómulo repeated:

"Yes, I'll give you the ultimate thing. The one and only and ultimate thing. Can't you see I'm quite willing to? I know the whole business, and I'm going into it more calmly and steadily than your husband did or your lover does."

But she was moaning like a child, and as Rómulo saw that blood and heard those moans he felt a hostile kind of pity. He put his hand to his belt, on the side where his militia knife hung. The duchess saw him do it and cried out with staring eyes:

"Don't kill me, Rómulo!"

Rómulo removed his hand from his belt and laid it near the pillow.

"You're leaving tomorrow. Your passport's downstairs, ready and waiting. You're leaving tomorrow, do you hear?"

"I?"

"Yes, you."

She moaned with her wounded mouth that was becoming inflamed:

"I think I'm ill, but I'll do whatever you like."

Rómulo could not look at her without feeling an immense compassion for her. He preferred to leave

211

rather than confess that compassion and went out backward, saying:

"You're not fooling me. I know it all and accept it. You're not fooling me. I'll give you the very last thing, but I'll only give it to you, not to him. To you, because I want to give it to you. I, without thinking of foolishness, without thinking of the people on other planets, as you say. Me. Do you hear? Me."

He came back again from the tower stairs. She told him she was grateful to him—with her wounded lip! —and only needed some sleep. Rómulo thought: "She's telling the truth." He also was telling it. And yet—he thought—they were both lying. Maybe up on that high level you could be comfortably, conveniently, and even virtuously above blood and fire. He, too, was above them, but his level was different. And there was nothing he could do now. Nothing except bow his head and offer it to her. Realizing she was afraid of him, he left without saying a word and went out with the help of his sticks.

He wanted to go down in the elevator so as to avoid the stairs, but ever since he had been shut in there with the dead man he had always avoided it whenever he could. And, just as he reached the staircase, he realized that everything was over. He was afraid of the captain's shoe on the stairs and justified his fear by thinking that, with his bandaged leg, it would be difficult to keep his balance if he stumbled. Then he turned back and headed for the elevator. He heard the duchess weeping. "Perhaps she's upset about the whole thing, my fate upsets her as well, and she takes it less calmly than I." This reflection moved him even more, and when he got into the elevator, for the first time he felt he was a real man—on the same level as the duchess —facing a really superhuman fate. The elevator was going down. The little carved prisms around the mirror, with their twinkling iridescent colors, gave off small blue flames like will-o'-the-wisps, that seemed full of allusions to the captain's body. When the elevator reached the ground floor, he stepped out, unconcerned as to whether he was seen or not. Luckily there was nobody about. He went to his room and got into bed. It was a long while before he fell asleep, thinking that this was his last night and his last sleep.

Rather late in the morning—after nine—he felt himself being shaken by the arm. It was the taciturn militiaman, telling him:

"The beautiful stranger's gone. She must be on her way to Valencia by now." And he added with enormous disappointment: "She's crazy. She told me it was General Miaja who murdered the captain." Cartridge laughed and added: "Well, she's crazy, but she was right about the furnaces. Sometimes crazy people get hunches like that."

Rómulo lay with his gaze suspended unblinkingly in the air. The militiaman added:

"When I told her it couldn't have been General

Miaja, she said I was right; she said Miaja only gave the order, and it was a priest that killed him."

"But you say she's gone?"

The militiaman thought Rómulo must still be half asleep. He clapped his hands to wake him up and then went off, saying he was going to the furnaces and would wait for him there, since he needed his help. Rómulo rose and went out to the park with his sticks, repeating in dazed wonder: "General Miaja. A priest." He looked forlornly at the tower, telling himself with dull pain: "There's nobody in there any more." And he could not feel grateful to the duchess for those wild words she had said to Cartridge, even though she had apparently wanted to save him by them. He felt grateful instead for the look and the voice with which she had said, the previous night, "Don't kill me." He went slowly over to the furnaces and sat down on the stone bench against the wall. Cartridge began enthusiastically showing him more incriminating articles, and Rómulo said to himself: "She tried to save me, in her own way." Cartridge went on showing him proofs. Rómulo did not feel they were at all dangerous. Or, rather, he saw the danger and did not bother about it.

"You say she's gone?"

"Of course."

Rómulo held his peace.

"And was she beautiful?"

"So beautiful that I felt suspicious the first day."

"Suspicious of what?"

"I don't know."

"Is it only the other side that has beautiful women?"

Cartridge did not understand. He went on showing Rómulo his finds. The latter asked:

"Did she have a sore on her upper lip?"

Cartridge replied mechanically that she had, and showed him new articles found in the furnaces. At last they began shouting loudly for Cartridge, and the militiaman went off, saying he had to go on duty. Rómulo was left alone, gazing at the top of a pine against the sky, gray now but of a gleaming grayness. Among the fronds of diminutive green needles, he could see a few black cones. Rómulo sat looking at the tracery of the pine needles against the sky. Sometimes a light breeze disturbed the pattern of the tracery. Sometimes, also, the fine needles were shaken by vibrations from the artillery. Two of the militiamen were still working busily on the lawn, and one of the craters had already been filled in and the earth leveled down. There was not a single bird.

Rómulo kept thinking about the duchess. Perhaps she had meant to tell the sentry that rubbish from the very beginning. But then why had she spoken to Cartridge the first day—two days ago—about the burnt body in the furnace? He did not want to think about that again. He liked the idea that in Valencia she was farther away from the front and the firing, but he had read that Valencia was still being bombed by the aviation every day. The duchess might be frightened, and she was all alone. For ever since the scene when Rómulo had made the puppets talk, he had felt sure she would be frightened the same as other people, and would suffer and weep like any ordinary woman. He was oppressed by the thought of the duchess fleeing, alone and panic-stricken.

He wandered about in the park all day. The militiaman came looking for him with new discoveries, and Rómulo asked him crossly:

"And what are you going to do with this collection of clues? Put them in a showcase?"

The militiaman said he was going to Police Headquarters next day. Rómulo retired to his room shortly afterward. "I can't go to Valencia until my leg's healed." But he felt sure he would go some day and find the duchess there. Still, the best way to obtain a passport was by speculating on the wounds in his leg.

He went to the cellar and found Midge as colorless as a wax figure, breathing asthmatically, and filthy in his rags. Rómulo stood looking at him in silence, as though he had never seen him before, and then asked him:

"What are you doing here?"

The midget delayed answering, and when he finally did so it was in the same haughty tones as on previous occasions:

"Chrissie's dead. I strangled her with these very hands."

He showed them to him with their fingers clenched. Rómulo told him that he could not stay there because he would die and suggested his going out in the park at once and putting a stop to all his fears and precautions. The midget swore he was not afraid and never had been, and he showed a readiness to go out but asked for assurances. Rómulo did not understand what he meant by this. He was becoming impatient.

"You can't stay in here. The cellar stinks already, and I don't want you to end up by infecting the air. Go on out ahead of me."

Rómulo's tone tolerated no reply, and the midget obeyed him. On the way, seeing Rómulo's bandages, he asked what had happened to him, but Rómulo did not answer. Rómulo was telling himself that, since the duchess was not in the palace, the dwarf would be able to come and go without the risk of her seeing him (he would have wished to spare her that sorry sight). Before going out, the midget said:

"Her Grace the duchess saw me here and made no objections. On the contrary, you would have thought she was pleased with my services."

Rómulo made him swear not to tell anyone about having been hidden in the cellars and exaggerated the danger of doing so. Just the same, Rómulo feared the midget might be capable of risking his life for the sake of boasting.

The midget's presence in the park was joyfully welcomed. The militiamen adopted him at once. When the midget was referring to Rómulo, he would say, "the gentleman." And when speaking of the duke and duchess, "Their Graces." This amused the soldiers of the guard even more. When Rómulo saw they accepted him unreservedly, he told them to be careful of him.

"Why?"

"He's a Fascist."

The idea of having this individual for an enemy put the finishing touch to the militiamen's glee. Realizing his opinions did not offend them, the midget spent his time boasting of them, perhaps from mere buffoonery.

Rómulo mounted the tower stairs to look for the captain's shoe, which might prove incriminating if the police came and made a search. When he found it, he was so near the duchess' rooms that he could not resist the temptation of going in. The midget, who sometimes felt he was in danger away from Rómulo, stuck close to him and followed him about like a dog. The hall was deserted, and the puppets lay sprawled on the carpet. Rain and wind were blowing in through the glassless windows. There was a desolate chill and silence about. The pictures on the walls gleamed more than ever, and the silence wounded him more deeply all the time. He saw some papers on the little table where the duchess occasionally used to write. He walked over to see if there was anything for him but found nothing. The midget scurried about, sticking his nose into everything with meddlesome readiness. In a still open book whose pages were half filled with

the duchess' handwriting, Rómulo read: "The 'devil'
hasn't come back any more. Perhaps they've killed
him." Who was the "devil"? Rómulo felt sure it was
her lover. He returned to the elevator with the shoe in
his hand but then threw it back carelessly onto the
divan and went away. The midget watched these ma-
neuvers without understanding them and without asking questions.

Rómulo could not sleep, and insomnia made him
thin. The militiamen had asked him several times
what was the matter with him. "Nothing," Rómulo
would say. "My wounds aren't healing properly."
This was the truth. The doctor was puzzled and took
an extract of his blood to be analyzed, but Rómulo
told himself he could not get well while this anguish
kept his flesh in a fever and his nerves in a constant
state of tension. The doctor gave him some sleeping
pills. Rómulo slept well for two nights and noticed
his wounds were beginning to heal at last. He gave
up his sticks. He grew used to his pain, and the anguish disappeared, giving place to constant depression. The bombardment of Madrid became heavier
during these days, and among other places destroyed
by the bombs was a school in which more than two
hundred children perished. Many photographs were
made of the little smashed bodies, photographs which
had a savagely expressive strength, and these were cir-

culated as propaganda. When they reached the militiamen's hands, the latter made indignant comments, but
Midge looked at the photos and contented himself with
saying:

"They've gone to heaven. The little angels have
gone to heaven."

Rómulo went about the park without speaking to
anybody. He had handed over the cellar keys to a new
officer, who was fetching the bottles up by dozens to be
sent to the front or to the hospitals. It was all being
done without consulting Rómulo, but in any case he
did not want to know anything about it.

The police had come in response to Cartridge's de-
nunciations but had merely drawn up a record of his
accusations and passed it on to the "Special Service
Division." Rómulo's statement was not given any
more prominence than the others.

López would ask Midge:

"If the Fascists entered Madrid, would you use
your influence to get me hanged?"

The dwarf arranged his pants:

"Strict justice will be done. Not vengeance, but justice."

Cartridge could not stand the midget and did not
conceal his aversion. Midge realized it and showed
himself more obsequious toward him than toward the
others. Referring to him, he would say the same thing
he used to say about Rómulo, that he was a gentleman.

Before going to bed at night, Midge would care-fully fill up the breaches left by the explosions in the garage door on the night of the bombardment.

Rómulo had now recovered completely and was waiting for the military passport for which he had applied. He thought of the duchess as a splendid promise that was fixed in time. Meanwhile, he worked in the gardens, helping the militiamen. The park was fairly mangled in the section near his old lodgings. The militiamen carted the earth in wheelbarrows with dolefully squeaking axles. Rómulo counted the hours that—according to his calculations—were left until his passport arrived. He had confused and contra-dictory presentiments about it, which he ascribed to the gray sky that covered the city day after day. There had been no sunshine since the duchess left. He felt groggy and bewildered. By the end of the afternoon he was so much on edge that he could not endure the squeaking of the barrow wheel and went to oil it.

Like the scars on Rómulo's legs, the garden's wounds had healed. From time to time Rómulo would go to his room, sit down on his bed, and remain staring at the wall.

The midget did not leave the palace much, but as soon as he poked his head into the street, some urchin or other would be sure to push curiosity to an imper-tinent extreme. The midget knew this and was always on his guard. Two eleven-year-old rascals used to sing, whenever they saw him:

221

"To have a little fun
I got married to a midget.
I put the bed up high,
And so he couldn't reach it."

The slyness of the song, and the innocence with which
they sang it, made an odd contrast. The dwarf would
answer:

"Why don't you go to school? Schools are getting
very interesting these days."

And he would laugh with a short guttural chuckle.

One day the midget said to Rómulo: "Do you know,
Gimlet looks for me at night?" And he showed him a
knife that he wore in his belt as a precaution. Rómulo
walked off without answering. The idea of a rat's wanting revenge seemed a piece of foolish madness to
Rómulo. Sometimes, when he thought the midget
might be crazy, he was afraid of his indiscretions,
especially of the possibility of his talking some day
about the duchess.

The field kitchen arrived, and the soldiers were getting ready to eat. Rómulo was not hungry and wandered slowly away to a bench in the main avenue,
where he sat down. At the end of the avenue there was
a scrap of paper lying on the ground, and the wind
kept flapping it up on one side and then letting it fall
again. The sight gave Rómulo a sensation of anguished
remoteness. Rómulo was thinking: "She never really
reproached me for being against her people." And a

222

little later: "She didn't get offended, either, when I spoke well of the militiamen. On that other level she and I know about, such things aren't important."

He went on waiting for the passport. The cold soon came, and the grass began to dry up. To burn up. Why should cold burn? But the winter cold gives the grass a fever. Is that how cold burns? Causing a fever in the grass, a fire at root and core, as with people? There is a cold that burns. Rómulo felt it, and he told himself the duchess' disappearance had brought this cold to the park, to the palace, and even to his peasant's bones, inured as they were to chill. But he would go after the duchess. The passport might arrive at any moment. Rómulo was thinking about all this while he went on watering the park. Halfway through the afternoon, he heard Ortiz' querulous voice:

"Leave that hose alone, Rómulo, or you'll have us all turning into frogs."

Rómulo shut off the faucet and, leaving the hose on the lawn like a dead snake, went toward the palace without saying anything. He called the Evacuation Commissariat on the telephone and asked about his passport. They answered that as he was of military age he could not leave Madrid. Rómulo hung up, greatly disappointed. He went into the ground-floor rooms of the tower. As he entered, he was thinking, although with no sensation of mystery, of the apparitions Balbina had told him about. He thought of the thin blue flame flickering in the center of the room

223

and especially remembered that voice the maids said they had heard: "I'm thirsty." This exclamation— "I'm thirsty"—seemed quite natural to Rómulo. He could understand that the mother duchess might be thirsty after death on account of the burning cold.

Rómulo spent all the first part of the night in the bedroom, and then, wanting to breathe the same air the duchess had breathed, he climbed the inner staircase to the second floor. The darkened anteroom received him as before, with its chill air that also had a feverish core. The puppets were still scattered about with enormously alive expressions. Rómulo felt his way over in the dark and turned on a lamp in one corner. The door at the end was open, and the darkness in the bedroom seemed frozen. Queen Hypotenuse was lying face downward on the divan, peering over the edge as though she wanted to see what the other dolls were doing on the carpet. With his back turned to the bedroom door, Rómulo thought he heard a patter of bare feet. At the same time a human voice whispered, just like the mother duchess' ghost:

"I'm thirsty."

Rómulo turned around and saw the duchess in a long white nightgown. Rómulo managed to ask:

"What did you say?"

The figure halted between the bedroom door and the bathroom and said in a low voice:

"I'm thirsty."

The duchess was opening and shutting her mouth,

which looked hot and dry. Rómulo went into the bathroom—the duchess seemed unable to find the door—filled a glass, and came out again. The duchess was no longer there. Rómulo stood with the glass in his hand, staring toward the bedroom, where the same white shape appeared to be flitting about. Rómulo entered and turned on the light. The disorder in the bedroom was startling, and all at once it made Rómulo realize that the ghost was the duchess herself, who had not gone to Valencia but had been lying here ill and abandoned for several weeks. The bedclothes had fallen onto the floor. The fur coat, bundled into a dark heap at the foot of the bed, looked like a huddled motionless bear. The bedroom was freezing, and the wind moaned in slight gusts through the broken panes.

Unaware of what she was doing, the duchess pulled the nightgown off one shoulder and revealed a naked breast. It seemed impossible that amidst so much misery that breast should still be young and fragrant. And her lack of modesty was not scorn, as it had been on other occasions. It was fever, the cold that burns. It was delirium, and Rómulo was in it, too, with his mute pale face. He stared at her without approaching. He saw her upper lip still inflamed, and the wound, small and dry, on a face that seemed transparent.

Rómulo stretched the glass out to her with a shaking hand, and she took it awkwardly and, as she drank, spilled more than half of it down her chest. She appeared not to feel the chill of the wet nightgown stick-

225

ing to her other breast. After drinking, she felt her
way over to the bed, muttering jumbled words. When
she found it, she let go of the glass, which rolled along
it and fell noiselessly onto the carpet. She lay down,
dragged one corner of the sheet over her, leaving her
legs and half the upper part of her body uncovered,
and closed her eyes, saying:

"My hair."

The duchess went on talking with her eyes shut.
Rómulo heard her say: "I'm not hungry." Rómulo
covered her body compassionately. Everything was
cold—the sheets, the blankets, the fur coat. Everything except her body, which was burning. Rómulo's
hand brushed against her bare thigh twice, and she
said:

"Yes, Estéban. I'm quite all right, Estéban."

For the first time, Rómulo was seeing her morally
defenseless, unresisting, humble, and forsaken. Hearing Estéban's name he pricked up his ears, but she
said nothing more. Rómulo seemed to have forgotten
the duchess' plight. He wanted to know, and she did
not speak. He was thinking: "In her delirium, it's not
the duke's name she says, but another's. Perhaps her
lover's."

He drew nearer.

"My Lady. . . ."

He called her again, entreatingly. His voice was so
full of tenderness that the duchess heard it and said,
almost smiling:

"Don't think I'm going to die. I'm quite all right."

Then she said Estéban's name again, and Rómulo went over to one corner of the parlor and sat down in an armchair. He watched her from there without thinking about anything. He could see the nickel-plated head of the bed, with its perpendicular bars that looked like glass. And at regular intervals he could hear a sharp little noise (like two small metal articles persistently clicking together) coming from there, from the headboard. He got up and went over. He saw the stopper of a hot-water bottle knocking almost imperceptibly against the bars, over and over again.

Rómulo did not know what to put it down to, but presently he realized the sick woman's heart-beats were making the bed quiver and causing this slight continuous bumping. He noticed the bottle was cold. He went to the bathroom, heated some water, replenished the bottle, and came back to her with it hot. He had found a phial of aspirin tablets in the bathroom, and he gave the duchess two with a glass of hot water. Soon afterward the duchess' breathing seemed to grow quieter. Yet Rómulo did not know whether she was sleeping or dying. "She didn't deceive me," he repeated like an obsession. "She didn't go to Valencia." She had not wanted to escape. He sat down again in his corner and went on looking at her in silence. "Maybe she's sleeping, maybe she's sleeping and will wake up again in her right mind, once she's had some rest."

227

Two or three hours went by in this way. When Rómulo thought of fetching a doctor, he realized it was past midnight and it would not be easy to find one. Besides, what could be better for her than sleep? And Rómulo remembered: "She began getting ill that day I made the puppets talk."

Thinking thus, Rómulo stared at the ceiling, the walls. After midnight, he heard the bombardment getting heavier. He enjoyed this fury of fire and explosions, this desperation in the dark which seemed as though it would blot out the life of the universe. Rómulo went over to the bed and sat down on it. A few shells burst near by. The explosions woke the duchess, who opened her eyes and turned them on Rómulo with a vague and distant look.

"Rómulo, why did you go away?"

She sat up.

"Give me a mirror, Rómulo."

Rómulo was staring stupidly at one of the mother-of-pearl designs representing a king and a queen, with a Gothic inscription at the foot, inlaid in the wood of the little table. He got up and fetched her a mirror; but she did not want it by then.

"Listen to me, Rómulo."

A moment later she repeated the same thing: "Listen to me, Rómulo," and then said nothing. She drew herself further up. She leaned her head on Rómulo's chest and said with growing weariness: "Rómulo, you . . . you're the first man I've ever known in all my life."

228

Rómulo thought he could hear the dolls, the puppets, raising a hubbub in the doorway, and when the duchess said: "Why are they shouting like that?" Rómulo was startled by the coincidence. The duchess kissed Rómulo's hand and said:

"Forgive me, Rómulo."

Rómulo had the impression she was gone. And it was true. Rómulo kissed her on the mouth and then said to her: "Why now? When I went to draw the dagger, you looked at me with the same look as tonight. Ever since then, I've known you were mine. You believe in me now. I know you do, but why now? Why only now? Because I wounded you, because I left you? Does it have to be that way? Am I only to have you that way? When you no longer have yourself? Why? Is it the law? The ancient law?" He kissed her again. Her mouth was still warm. "What are you now? Where are you?"

He spoke to himself, but, in the hope that she might still be able to hear him, he raised his voice:

"What kind of a law is this? Are God's laws only for the world of the dead?"

Nobody answered him. He saw the midget in the doorway. The midget was staring at the room, at the bed, with an expression of terror.

"Is it Her Grace, the duchess?"

Rómulo made no reply, and the midget entered on tiptoe.

"Has she expired?"

Rómulo stood up and said to him:

"You've seen nothing, eh? If you say a word about this, I'll rip out your tongue."

Midge had a feeling that Rómulo had killed the duchess and that was why he was threatening him. Rómulo realized it.

"She died, but nobody knows or must know that she's here."

The midget could not resign himself to a passive attitude.

"What'll we do with the body?"

As so often before, Rómulo did not answer him, and the midget replied to his own question:

"I'll stay on guard at the door."

For a moment, Rómulo thought he heard the puppets squealing again in the next room. They were not squealing like human beings, or like puppets, or like chickens, or like rabbits—not even like rats—but like mischievous little sprites. Aunt Misery was singing:

"Ring-around the roses, a pocketful of posies, old blood, new blood, we all fall down. And the law of the world, that runs and always loses."

Uncle Babu repeated:

"Everyone to the ransom of youth, from the cradle to death." Then he gave a roar of laughter.

Queen Hypotenuse seemed to be looking at the same motif of a king and queen of mother-of-pearl inlaid in the lower part of a bureau and added: "And from the shadows to the great light."

Rómulo did not know whether he had heard "the great light," or "the great night," or the blight or the plight or the fight or perhaps the kite or the bite. . . .

"I'll stay here, keeping watch."

It was the midget. Rómulo glanced at him without comprehending, and the midget explained:

"The rats'll come up. They're sure to come up. But I'll answer for the duchess' body."

Rómulo was gazing at that body. What purity there was in the mystery of her half-opened eyes and mouth! He saw another puppet on the threshold. This time it was not the Queen, but the judge, Don Requirements, who also seemed to be getting back his own youth by crying:

"*Acta est fabula!*"